Off Off Broadway
26th Se...

Selected by New York theatre critics, professionals, and the editorial staff of Samuel French, Inc. as the most important plays of the Twenty-Sixth Annual Off Off Broadway Original Short Play Festival sponsored by Love Creek Productions.

TICKETS, PLEASE!
by Anthony Sportiello

SOMEPLACE WARM
by Peter Macklin

THE TEST
by Paula J. Caplan

A CLOSER LOOK
by Arlene Hutton

A PEACE REPLACED
by Brian Maloney

THREE TABLES
by Dan Remmes

A SAMUEL FRENCH ACTING EDITION

SAMUEL FRENCH
FOUNDED 1830

SAMUELFRENCH.COM

MUSIC USE NOTE

Licensees are solely responsible for obtaining formal written permission from copyright owners to use copyrighted music in the performance of this play and are strongly cautioned to do so. If no such permission is obtained by the licensee, then the licensee must use only original music that the licensee owns and controls. Licensees are solely responsible and liable for all music clearances and shall indemnify the copyright owners of the play and their licensing agent, Samuel French, Inc., against any costs, expenses, losses and liabilities arising from the use of music by licensees.

IMPORTANT BILLING AND CREDIT REQUIREMENTS

All producers of *TICKETS, PLEASE!, SOMEPLACE WARM, THE TEST, A CLOSER LOOK, A PEACE REPLACED,* and *THREE TABLES must* give credit to the Author of the Play in all programs distributed in connection with performances of the Play, and in all instances in which the title of the Play appears for the purposes of advertising, publicizing or otherwise exploiting the Play and/or a production. The name of the Author *must* appear on a separate line on which no other name appears, immediately following the title and *must* appear in size of type not less than fifty percent of the size of the title type.

TABLE OF CONTENTS

TICKETS, PLEASE!

by

Antony Sportiello

TICKETS, PLEASE! was presented at The 42nd Street Workshop in May 2001 under the direction of Manfred Bormann with the following cast:

BARBARA...Susanna Fraser
TERRY...Mark Hofmaier

ABOUT THE AUTHOR

ANTONY SPORTIELLO is the author of several plays including *Second Chance, LOL, Waiting for Al, Absent Friends, Suicide Rings* and *National Pastime.*

CHARACTERS

BARBARA: a smart, successful business woman in her
   mid thirties
TERRY: a pleasant, genial, nicely dressed man

SETTING

Place: On board a New Jersey Transit train heading from
   Princeton to New York
Time: The present

(The scene is set on board the New Jersey Transit train heading from Princeton to New York. BARBARA WOODWARD enters what is currently an empty car, reading The Wall Street Journal. *She is a smart, successful business woman in her mid-thirties. She finds a seat. An item in the* Journal *catches her eye. She pulls out a cellular phone and dials a number.)*

BARBARA. *(On the phone.)* Hey, Jim, it's me. You see the piece in the *Journal* on Varnell? Yeah, that's what I thought. I'm telling you, they're ripe for the picking. So, who makes the first move?

(The CONDUCTOR enters.)

CONDUCTOR. Tickets, please.
BARBARA. *(Without even looking at him, she flashes a monthly pass. He checks it and exits to the next car.)* Ticker symbol's VN. Started the day at 75. By the end of next year, it'll be 100, maybe 110. It's a rocket, Jim, just like I told you it would be. But we're going to have to move fast. *(TERRY enters from the back. TERRY is a pleasant, genial fellow, dressed nicely. He notices BARBARA and sits across from her.)* Yeah, I know Charlie's hesitant. Charlie's always hesitant. Charlie would be hesitant to leave a burning building until the flames reached his ass. *(She notices TERRY. He smiles at her. She turns away.)* Look, this is just like Yahoo all over again. Do you remember how I begged him to get into that? Now where is it? And where are we? I mean, I don't know what I'm doing here if he's not going to listen to me. I could be making someone else rich. *(She looks at TERRY again. He's not smiling.)* Hold on, Jim. *(She puts the phone against her and talks to TERRY.)* Do you mind? This is a private call.
TERRY. Not anymore.
BARBARA. *(Muttering to herself.)* Oh, God, why do I get all the crazies. *(On the phone again.)* Look, Jim, I'm going to have to call you back. I may need to dial 911. Jim? Hello?
TERRY. Jim's not there, Barbara.
BARBARA. What the hell's wrong with this phone? *(Suddenly realizing.)* What did you say?
TERRY. I said, 'Jim's not there.'
BARBARA. No, you said, 'Jim's not there, Barbara.' How did you know my name?
TERRY. Don't be afraid.
BARBARA. I'll give you one shot before I yell for the conductor. Who are you, and what do you want?

TERRY. How've you been feeling lately, Barbara?

BARBARA. What?

TERRY. A little tired? Fatigued? How have your headaches been?

BARBARA. My headaches? What do you know of them? Who the hell are you?

TERRY. You wouldn't go see a doctor about them, would you? Not that it would have made any difference. You had one a while ago. A bad one. How is it now?

BARBARA. My head is fine. So are my vocal cords. Now, I'm going to count to three. One.

TERRY. I didn't want it to go like this.

BARBARA. Two.

TERRY. It's not fair to you, really.

BARBARA. Three.

(She opens her mouth to yell.)

TERRY. *(Gently.)* You're dead, Barbara.

BARBARA. *(Stops in shock.)* What did you say?

TERRY. I'm sorry. I usually don't like to come right out with it like that. I much prefer easing into it, getting you prepared. Unfortunately, I'm running late.

BARBARA. You said I'm dead. What is ... I mean ... is that some kind of sick joke?

TERRY. The truth is, you should have died before catching this train. But we're short staffed right now.

BARBARA. What are you talking about? Who are you?

TERRY. Call me Terry. It's short for Terrence.

BARBARA. What do you mean when you say, "I'm dead?'

TERRY. Well, it's pretty self-explanatory. It means your time is up. I've been sent here to collect you.

BARBARA. I want to know how you know my name.

TERRY. Barbara, please. We don't have time.

BARBARA. Oh, wait a minute. I get it. I get it! This is a joke, right? For my birthday! This is Jim pulling a joke. Oh, Christ. Oh, man, you had me going there for a second. I thought you were a lunatic.

TERRY. It's no joke.

BARBARA. He's getting back at me for the time I had the stripper show up at his in-laws. Oh, that maniac.

TERRY. Look out the window, Barbara. What do you see?

BARBARA. I've got to call him right now.

(She picks up the phone again.)

TERRY. The phone is dead, Barbara. So are you. Look out the window.

BARBARA. No.

TERRY. Why not?

BARBARA. I don't want to.

TERRY. You know I'm telling the truth. In your heart, you know I'm telling the truth. Now, please. Look out the window. *(Slowly, she does.)* What do you see?

BARBARA. Nothing.

TERRY. Exactly. No roads ... no lights ... no cars. That's because they're gone. Or, rather, you're gone. I'm very sorry. But it's your time. You know it, don't you?

BARBARA. Yes. I don't know why, but ... I don't understand. How ...

TERRY. How did it happen? *(She nods.)* The headaches. A blood vessel burst in your brain. There was nothing you could have done.

BARBARA. But they weren't that bad.

TERRY. You must have a high threshold for pain. Now, are you ready?

BARBARA. No, I'm not ready! You walk in here, tell me I'm dead, and expect me to be ready?

TERRY. *(Looking at his watch.)* I understand yow you feel, but ....

BARBARA. You don't know how I feel! You don't know how I feel at all!

TERRY. I'm sorry. I know it's a shock. But I'm really way behind schedule. I have to move it along.

BARBARA.. Ready for what? I mean, how do you ... what happens now?

TERRY. We leave. I escort you to a temporary holding shelter, you'll be duly processed, and then you'll proceed.

BARBARA. Proceed to where?

TERRY. I'm sorry, I couldn't tell you even if I knew. Which I don't. Now, please. I really am behind.

BARBARA. Oh, God. I don't believe this.

TERRY. Barbara, relax. I think you're going to be pleasantly surprised. Now, please. Take a deep breath and sit back. It'll be over before you know it.

BARBARA. I don't have time for one last phone call?

TERRY. I don't have time! Now, I'm sorry. I really must insist.

BARBARA. All right.

(She takes a deep breath and sits back.)

TERRY. Good girl. Tell me, why did you think Jim would be doing this for your birthday? Your birthday's not for months.

BARBARA. My birthday is two days away.

TERRY. *(Stopped short.)* What?

BARBARA. I said, my birthday is two days away.

TERRY. No, it isn't.

BARBARA. It isn't?

TERRY. No, your birthday is in February.

BARBARA. No, my birthday is in August.

TERRY. I'm telling you it's in February.

BARBARA. Look, you want to see my driver's license?

TERRY. *(Suddenly suspicious.)* Wait a minute. *(Pause.)* What train is this?

BARBARA. What?

TERRY. The train. What train is it?

BARBARA. It's the New Jersey Transit, heading to Elizabeth.

TERRY. *To* Elizabeth?! Not *away* from?!

BARBARA. No.

TERRY. Oh, Christ.

BARBARA. What's the matter?

TERRY. *(Screaming up to the skies.)* You morons!! You put me on the wrong train!!

BARBARA. What are you talking about?

TERRY. Is your name Barbara Louise Woodward?

BARBARA. No. It's Barbara Theresa Woodward.

TERRY. Oh, hell.

BARBARA. Are you saying I'm not dead?

TERRY. No, you're not dead. But I am. *(Up to the skies again.)* Idiots! Don't they have maps up there?!

BARBARA. *(Looking out the window.)* I can see lights again! And cars!

TERRY. *(Sourly.)* Congratulations. I'm very happy for you.

BARBARA. My heart. My heart is beating so fast. God, you had me so scared!

TERRY. I am sorry about that. Don't worry. When I leave, I'll take all memory of this with me. You won't remember anything about it.

BARBARA. Oh, God. Oh, sweet Jesus. I was dead. For about three minutes, I was actually dead. Oh, man. Talk about a wake-up call. Let me just catch my breath again. Has this ever happened to you before?

TERRY. It happens. No often, but … especially when you have two people with the same name in the same area. That's when it gets confusing. Between you and me, it's those damn computers. Modern technology, my ass. It was easier in the old days.

BARBARA. Oh, good Lord. *(Takes deep breaths.)* So, tell me. What about the other Barbara Woodward? The one with the blood vessel?

TERRY. Oh, someone else will get her. *(Looks at his watch.)* Probably already has. Harold, I'll bet. That'd be his shift.

BARBARA. Poor girl.

TERRY. I'm telling you, it's not that bad. But you won't find out for a while yet.

BARBARA. Thank God for that. *(Pause. He sits back.)* Well?

TERRY. Well, what?

BARBARA. I don't mean to be rude, but don't you need to be going?

TERRY. Yes, I do. Care to tell me how?

BARBARA. I don't know. Can't you just fly or something?

TERRY. No, I can't fly. Who do you think I am, Peter Pan?

BARBARA. Oh.

TERRY. Hell, I even had to pay for my ticket.

BARBARA. I'm sorry, I just thought ... I mean, you made an entire train disappear!

TERRY. I didn't make anything disappear. I just changed your perspective. That's an entirely different matter.

BARBARA. Oh.

TERRY. You sound disappointed.

BARBARA. Well ... a little, maybe. Look, I don't care. I'm just happy to be alive.

TERRY. Do you want to get back to your phone call?

BARBARA. Hmmm? Oh, him. He can wait. It's just business.

TERRY. Oh.

(He takes out a notebook, looks at it and frowns.)

BARBARA. What? What is it?

TERRY. Your life is just business, isn't it, Barbara?

BARBARA. What do you mean?

TERRY. Barbara Theresa Woodward, born August 12th, 1962, New Orleans, Louisiana. Graduated first in her class at Vassar, business major, hired immediately by RJR Nabisco to head up the foods division. Salary, seventy-five thousand dollars a year. Left RJR for Shearson Lehman, got into merchant banking. Salary, one hundred and thirty-five thousand a year, plus apartment, plus expense account, plus a Ferrari. Speaking of which ....

BARBARA. It's in the shop. Go on. What else?

TERRY. Parents dead, one sister living in Connecticut. Barbara herself is single. Wants no kids. Wants lovers, though, and has them. At the moment there are three. All of them wealthy, all of them successful, all of them ...

BARBARA. Married.

TERRY. Indeed. Works thirteen hours a day, six days a week, twelve months a year. Last had a vacation in '98.

TERRY. That's pretty impressive for someone who got on the

wrong train.

TERRY. Give me a specific name and I can give you an entire history. The thing is, a few minutes ago you were scared you were going do die. Now, as I look back over your file, I wonder why.

BARBARA. Are you serious?

TERRY. No offense, but what have you done with your life that makes it worth holding onto?

BARBARA. I'll have you know I'm one of the most successful business women in the Northeast. I have a condo, a house in the Hamptons, my Ferrari ....

TERRY. Your sister has two kids, ages nine and five. Jenny and Taylor. On your sister's wall is a picture of her and Jenny. The nine-year-old has her arms around your sister's neck and is giving her a kiss.

BARBARA. That's dynamite. Exactly what is your point?

TERRY. My point is, I'll trade you that picture for your condo, your house, and your Ferrari. I'll trade you that moment with Jenny for all your stocks, your bonds and your mutual funds. If you have half a brain, you'll take it and consider yourself lucky.

BARBARA. You can't seriously put all I've done up against the raising of two kids on forty-five thousand dollars a year. She works in a bookstore, for Christ sake! They live in a hovel!

TERRY. Your sister is loved, Barbara. Deeply loved. By a husband and two beautiful children, at least. Are you? If this was truly your time, if I had not made a mistake, what good would all your money have done you? Gotten you a bigger funeral?

BARBARA. Don't say that. I'm loved.

TERRY. Oh, you are? By who?

BARBARA. By lots of people.

TERRY. Name one. Your married boyfriends? What they loved in you they'll quickly learn to love in another. Go on, Barbara. Give me one name.

BARBARA. My sister loves me.

TERRY. Yes. She does. One other name.

BARBARA. Well, there's ... I mean, I'm sure in time ... look, there's more to life than that. I do a good job, I make a good salary. I've worked hard for it. I'm not going to feel guilty about that.

TERRY. Yes, you will. Thirty years from now you're going to be sitting in a beautifully furnished apartment, surrounded by expensive belongings, hand-picked from a catalogue. You're going to stare out your window overlooking Central Park, down at the people who are out there laughing and playing, and you're going to weep because you're so alone. You're going to cry, and you're going to cry, and you're not going to stop for days. See, in the bigger picture, Barb, your sister's a hell of a lot richer than you are.

BARBARA. *(Pause. Softly.)* Why are you doing this?

TERRY. I'm sorry. I should know better by now. Ten centuries in this business and I still never learn.

BARBARA. Learn what?

TERRY. Learn that it's unfair. That sometimes the whole damn business doesn't make any sense.

BARBARA. You're the one not making any sense. Why are you so angry at me? And why do you keep bringing up my sister?

TERRY. Because she's going to die. Soon, I can tell you because you won't remember it any way, but in two months your sister's going to cross the street to get a newspaper and get hit by a drunk driver running a red light.

BARBARA. No.

TERRY. Your brother-in-law's going to try his best but soon he'll find that he can't hold down a job and take care of two young kids. He'll ask you for a loan but you'll turn him down figuring, rightly so, that he won't be good for it. Jenny will wind up with his parents. He'll hold on to Taylor for a little while, but eventually, Taylor will run away. They'll put him in a foster home. Ten years from now, your brother-in-law commits suicide in a trailer park.

BARBARA. No!

TERRY. On the bright side, in those same ten years, you'll increase your portfolio by a wide margin, investing in a diverse number of highly successful stocks and bonds, not to mention your annual salary, which will climb to well over five hundred thousand dollars a year. You'll have two Ferrari's, an even larger condo in Manhattan and real estate in the French Riviera. So all told, I guess it's a happy ending.

BARBARA. *(Emotionally.)* You're a goddamn son of a bitch.

TERRY. No, I'm just a man with a lousy job. But don't worry about it, Barbara Theresa Woodward. Once I leave this train your memory of this entire conversation will be erased. You'll have no guilty conscience to worry about.

BARBARA. Fine with me. I don't need this shit. As for you, you can rot in hell.

TERRY. I can see the future, and that's not likely.

BARBARA. Screw you, Terrence. *(She starts out, then stops.)* Let me ask you something.

TERRY. Go ahead.

BARBARA. What if I don't forget?

TERRY. Say what?

BARBARA. If you make me forget, all the things you've just said will come to pass.

TERRY. They'll come to pass anyway.

BARBARA. Not necessarily. If you let me remember, I can

change it. I can make sure she never crosses that street. I can use my money to move them to a better neighborhood, a bigger house, I can do it tomorrow.

TERRY. That's your solution for everything, isn't it, Barb? Throw enough money at it and the problem goes away. Not this time. Your sister's going to die, you're going to live and that's the way it is.

BARBARA. What do you want me to do?

TERRY. Feel lousy about it. Like I do. The difference is, in two minutes you'll stop feeling lousy. Whereas I'll feel like this for a while.

BARBARA. Good. You should. It's your fault.

TERRY. My fault?

BARBARA. I can save them. I can change things. But you won't let me.

TERRY. Why would you want to do that? Where's the return? Look, Barb, your soul's not in danger. This isn't an Ebeneezer Scrooge type of thing. Keep going like you're going and it won't be held against you. I promise.

BARBARA. What if I don't want to keep going like I'm going? Damn it, you can't open my eyes to this and then just turn the lights out again!

TERRY. What do you expect me to do?

BARBARA. Let me remember.

TERRY. I can't do that.

BARBARA. You can do it. I know you can.

TERRRY. It's totally against the rules. In fact, there's only one rule and that's it.

BARBARA. Listen to me. I didn't ask you to come here. I didn't send you to the wrong train. That was your screw-up. But you now have a chance to do some good, to save lives instead of taking them. Mine included. Try to see the forest for the trees. I mean, there's an upside for everyone here if you just ....

TERRY. Barbara, this isn't one of your business deals. I'm not impressed by your logic, or your fine analytic reasoning. You want something from me, it better come from the heart. Not the head.

BARBARA. *(Softly.)* All right. Do you want to know who I was going to call back when I thought I was dead? My sister. And do you want to know why? Because the last time I can remember being happy was when I was with her. Growing up, she took care of me. Protected me. Loved me. I owe her everything. Please. I'm begging you. Don't let me leave this train not knowing. I'm not strong enough to do it on my own. I know that. But if you let me keep this, I can change. Not overnight, but little by little, I can change. I can save them. And I want to. I want to very, very much. Terry, please. Do this and I'll make you proud of me, I swear I will. And next time, when you come to get me, you won't have to ask who loves me.

TERRY. Barbara ....

BARBARA. Please, Terry. God in heaven, please.

TERRY. *(Takes a deep breath.)* Get out.

BARBARA. What?

TERRY. The train's stopped. Get out.

BARBARA. Will I ...?

TERRY. Yes. You'll remember. Now, get out. *(BARBARA starts out, then comes back and hugs TERRY. She leaves. He gets up, then looks up at the sky. He smiles.)* Mission accomplished. See you on the flip side.

(TERRY winks and leaves.)

END OF THE PLAY

SOMEPLACE WARM

by

Peter Macklin

Special Thanks:

Steven McElroy, Tina Howe,
Marie and Folasade Augustin-Glave,
Abby Lindsay, Megan Wills, Paul Adams
and all the Emerging Artists

SOMEPLACE WARM was presented by Emerging Artists Theatre in August, 2001 under the direction of Steven McElroy with the following cast:

MARIE...Kim Ders

DOCTOR...Kurt Kingsley

MAX...Carter Inskeep

STEVEN...Walker Richards

CLAIRE..Rebecca Hoodwin

ABOUT THE AUTHOR

Also an actor, PETER MACKLIN has performed in many New York City venues. He is currently a candidate for an M.F.A. in acting from the Alabama Shakespeare Festival/University of Alabama. He is at this time writing another play about social and racial politics in the South which is, as of yet, untitled. *Someplace Warm* is his first play.

CHARACTERS

MARIE: Thirty-one year-old woman. White.
MAX: Forty-four year-old man. White.
STEVEN: Forty year-old man. Max's husband. Black.
CLAIRE: Fifty-one year-old woman. Marie's mother. White.
DOCTOR: Sixty-five year-old man. White.

SETTING

Place: An abortion clinic. Other settings as indicated.
Time: The present.

(Present day. Pre-op room of an abortion clinic in Heartland, U.S.A. MARIE is sitting down in a chair center stage. The DOCTOR is standing over her.)

MARIE. Please. I came here to do it. I want to do it.

DOCTOR. I'm sorry you are upset but the interview is common practice. In fact, it's the law here. Are you sure you want to terminate this pregnancy?

MARIE. Yes.

DOCTOR. Why?

MARIE. That's none of your business.

DOCTOR. We need to make sure you really want to do this.

MARIE. I sure picked the wrong place to get off the bus, hunh?

DOCTOR. Maybe. Maybe not. Tell me your story.

MARIE. I could lie you know.

DOCTOR. This is meant to benefit you. If you lie, it'll be your conscience. And your lost baby.

MARIE. If you don't like my story, you won't do it?

DOCTOR. Untrue. I'll do it if I despise your story. It's my job. This isn't about me. It's about you. This is your final chance to reconsider. Through these doors is a cold metal table covered with tissue paper that is supposed to make you feel comfortable while I reach a vacuum into your cervical canal and end your pregnancy. After this, there is no turning back. Go through it again. Maybe you'll find some hope.

MARIE. I'm not in New York anymore.

DOCTOR. No you're not. Well ...?

(Silence.)

MARIE. I invited them over .... *(Light change. We are now in MARIE's New York apartment. [This sort of change will happen often and will be the demarcation between scenes.] MAX and STEVEN have entered. MARIE is now addressing the two men.)* Thanks for coming.

MAX. Of course.

MARIE. Sorry I missed your birthday.

STEVEN. Please. It was more depressing than anything else.

MAX. Steven ....

STEVEN. What? You have a couple of years on me, sweets. I need time to adjust. I just don't get it. I was in my thirties a week ago. And now, BAM, I'm in my forties. I'm still not quite sure how that happened.

MAX. It's been forty years since that precious bald noggin of yours graced this planet. That's how it happened.

STEVEN. I feel like my father. Only I was eight when he turned forty. What have *I* done? Uch.... Come here the both of you, I need our famous three-way hug. If for no other reason, I need to be propped up.

(They do their famous three-way hug.)

MAX. So what's for dinner?

MARIE. Puttanesca.

STEVEN. What did you call me?

MARIE. Thanks again for coming. I needed the two of you.

STEVEN. I had a feeling that this wasn't just a casual dinner.

MARIE. No.

MAX. Before we start, I want to make a toast. *(Lifts up his wine glass.)* To the three of us. Partners in an insane world. *(STEVEN and MAX drink but MARIE doesn't. Mock insulted.)* You didn't like the toast?

MARIE. I'm pregnant.

(She cries.)

STEVEN. Holy Christ.

MAX. It's his?

MARIE. Of course it's his. I haven't ... you know ... since ....

STEVEN. No, we didn't think you did.

MAX. Have you made an appointment?

MARIE. To ....

MAX. Yes.

MARIE. No.

STEVEN. No?

MARIE. I'm thinking about ....

MAX. You're not!

MARIE. I am.

STEVEN. Are you sure that's what you want to do?

MARIE. No.

STEVEN. Then ....

MARIE. Is any one ever sure?

MAX. Is this a religious thing?

MARIE. Hell no.

MAX. You cried.

MARIE. Out of happiness.

STEVEN. You didn't seem too happy.

MARIE. And out of pain. Something good has to come out of evil.

STEVEN. That's the truth.

MAX. We'll be there for you.

STEVEN. Auntie Max and Auntie Steven.

MARIE. If I went through with it, I know you'd be there.

MAX. If anyone who has the right to ... to ... get rid of ... end the ... it's you.

MARIE. I want a family.

MAX. You have one. Where is she? Ohio?

MARIE. I don't talk to her.

STEVEN. You won't tell her?

MARIE. She doesn't need to know.

STEVEN. She might have something to say.

MARIE. She wouldn't. And if she did, I wouldn't hear her. She's in Ohio.

MAX. Would you do this alone?

MARIE. Just the baby and me. *(MAX and STEVEN share a look. MARIE stops the action. MAX and STEVEN freeze. To doctor.)* See that look, doc? Remember that look. They're communicating. They're saying, "This is our chance." I didn't see it then. But now I see it clear as day ....

(The action resumes.)

STEVEN. Just you and the baby? Here? In New York?

MARIE. I don't plan to leave.

STEVEN. It's expensive here.

MARIE. I know.

MAX. You'll have to work.

MARIE. I know.

STEVEN. You'll need a bigger place.

MARIE. I know.

MAX. Money for clothes.

MARIE. I kno.... Fine! So, I won't do it!

MAX. That's not what we mean.

MARIE. What do you mean?

STEVEN. *(MAX and STEVEN share a look. Then, to MARIE.)* Suppose we want to help.

MARIE. I know. Auntie Steven and Auntie Max.

MAX. Yes but ... how about an upgrade?

STEVEN. Daddy Steven and Daddy Max.

MAX. Or Daddy Max and Daddy Steven.

MARIE. With Mommy Marie?

STEVEN. Of course.

MARIE. I don't know. What would that mean exactly?

MAX. We'll be a lot more involved. You'll have a lot more help.

MARIE. But how do we ...?

MAX. We'll figure it out as we go.

STEVEN. We'll be a family.

MARIE. A family?

MAX. Yes.

MARIE. A family with three parents. Two of them a gay couple. The other a rape vic … *(Pause.)* survivor ….

MAX. Yeah, sounds crazy.

MARIE. My mother would flip.

STEVEN. Yeah.

MARIE. Let's do it. *(Back to abortion clinic.)* So, two weeks went by. The three of us lived our lives as our little family. And we loved it. I did and I know they did. I was part of a family. They were going to have the child that they so desperately wanted. Those two weeks, I wasn't a rape vic … survivor anymore. I was going to be a mother. And that scared the shit out of me. *(Pause.)* Max dragged us to FAO Schwarz. The big toy store.

(Lights and sound up on FAO Schwarz.)

STEVEN. I can't believe we're here.

MAX. I don't care. Tourist or not, I'm buying our baby a toy from here.

STEVEN. He won't even know. You could buy him a sock and he'll love it.

MAX. My child is not playing with a sock.

MARIE. Neither is mine. I was with you for a while Steven but now ….

STEVEN. All right, all right. *(Spots the G.I. Joe section.)* Holy shit! G. I Joe? The big ones? They still make those?

MAX. I think we have a convert.

MARIE. Are you sure he's forty?

MAX. I'm sure, but he's not.

STEVEN. If you two don't mind, I'm going over there. Where will you be?

MAX. Stuffed animals.

STEVEN. I'll see you there.

(STEVEN runs off to the G.I. Joe section.)

MARIE. G.I. Joe, hunh?

MAX. I've had to be a G.I. Joe so many times. Taking him into prison, handcuffing him …. Oooh, here's stuffed animals. That's what I want. That one. The big blue bear. *(Gets down on his knees and talks to MARIE's belly.)* You hear that little person?

(MAX kisses MARIE's belly. Light change; abortion clinic.)

MARIE. And that's where my Aunt Nellie saw us. By the big blue bear. She was in New York at a Girl Scouts of America Troupe Leader Convention. She was never in New York before and she wanted to see the singing clock that she's heard so much about in FAO Schwarz. Damn tourist trap. So she saw the three of us, followed us back to my apartment and then called my mother. Aunt Nellie never approached us. She never asked if I wanted to let my mother know where I was. *(Lights up on MARIE's apartment, there is a faint knock on the door. MARIE doesn't notice. Then a more confident knock.)* Who is it?

CLAIRE. Marie?

MARIE. Yes. Who is it?

CLAIRE. Marie. It's me.

MARIE. Who is ... . *(Realizing who it is.)* No ....

CLAIRE. Sweetheart? Aunt Nellie saw you in some toy store. She told me where you were.

MARIE. I don't want to see you. *(To herself.)* Fuck. Fuck.

CLAIRE. Please don't do this. I drove all the way from Ohio.

MARIE. You don't drive.

CLAIRE. I do now.

MARIE. Oh.

CLAIRE. Please open the door. It smells like pee out here. *(MARIE doesn't.)* I'm your mother, for pity's sake. Please. You must still .... Please. *(MARIE opens the door. CLAIRE walks in. Silence. Silence.)* This was probably the wrong thing to do. *(Starts to the door.)* I'm sorry. *(Stops at the door.)* It's just that I drove all the way from Ohio to be here. For someone who doesn't drive a lot, that's a long trip. But what could I do? I sure wasn't going to fly. That is the most unnatural way to travel. To be crammed in a metal can and projected three miles up in the air? No thank you. I'll tell you. All those plane crashes you see on the evening news. It's just creepy. But I guess anything on the evening news is creepy. They have a way of making you scared to even wake up in the morning. Why can't they have a news channel that only reports good things? The world would be a much better place. But that's not the way things go. It just seems to be too much at times. *(Noticing the bag she's holding.)* You know, on my way here, I stopped at, oh, about twenty-five McDonald's and such. I'm surprised I'm not three hundred pounds by now. Anyway, I stopped at so many because I tried to talk myself out of coming at each one. I couldn't when I was driving because I seem to go into a trance when I drive. But I would stop and try to tell myself not to come, that you probably don't want to see me. So I found myself at these McDonalds ordering the same thing, the Kid's Meal. Why? I don't know. I could say it was because I wanted to watch what I ate but then I would have ordered one of them salads, you know? I wouldn't have eaten the dressing though. I've heard the dressing is more fattening than the burgers. But I didn't eat a salad. I just kept on eating those Kid's Meals. I told the workers that my grandkid was waiting for me. I see now, looking at you, that glow, that I was right but they knew I didn't really know for sure. I could see it in their faces. This one teenage girl stared at me like I was crazy. She reminded me of you when you were that age. Who gave her the right to judge me? Just because she was on the other side of that counter! Freckles. Bouncy. Like she knew everything. *(Pause.)* I hate to lie. But I was embarrassed! But these meals. They were so cute. The little burgers, like an angel made them. The little fries, like they were made only for kids. And the little drink. Every time I thought I was going to order the, let's say Double Quarter Pounder with Extra Cheese, I would just come out and say "Kid's Meal, please." I took it as a sign. From God. That I should keep on going. Here. I found my determination from those meals. So, I have toys. Lots of Kid's Meal toys. I would like to give them to you. I drove all the way from Ohio to give them to you. Highway to highway. Turnpike to turnpike. To here. I was just trying to be thoughtful. Listen to me ramble. I know. I don't want to cause trouble. Please, *please*, take these toys. Maybe the baby would like them. You could tell the baby they're from it's grandma.

(She stands holding out the plastic McDonald's bag. Silence.)

MARIE. Nellie told you.

CLAIRE. My baby's having a baby.

MARIE. I didn't ask you to come.

CLAIRE. Let me take a look at you. *(Takes her in.)* You look the same.

MARIE. I didn't ask you to come.

CLAIRE. You're hair ….

MARIE. I know.

CLAIRE. I like it.

MARIE. You do?

CLAIRE. I do.

MARIE. You're just saying that.

CLAIRE. *(Clasping her hands together.)* Thank the Lord. It's true! My baby is having a baby.

MARIE. It's fat.

CLAIRE. I carried you. I know what it looks like when someone's with child.

MARIE. Aunt Nellie still has a big mouth, hunh? Ten years hasn't changed a thing has it?

CLAIRE. She knew I wanted to see you.

MARIE. You didn't come before.

CLAIRE. You didn't want me to.

MARIE. Who said?

CLAIRE. You ran out on *me*. No address. No information about anything.

MARIE. I wanted you to work towards something for a change.

CLAIRE. What?

MARIE. Forget it.

CLAIRE. *(Yells.)* How dare you!

MARIE. How dare I what?

CLAIRE. *(Pause.)* So, where's this husband of yours?

MARIE. What?

CLAIRE. Nellie told me that you were with a man who seemed to take good care of you ... and another man.

MARIE. I'm not married.

CLAIRE. Oh, Marie, you didn't.

MARIE. No Mom, I didn't. I was ... it's not important. *(To abortion clinic, lights down on CLAIRE.)* You see, my mother was the most religious, repressed subservient woman I knew. She had no mind of her own. I had to leave her. The last straw happened for me when I came home from senior year at Dartmouth. Winter break. Christmas. My father was divorcing her because he finally decided on another woman ....

(To ten years prior; CLAIRE's old house.)

CLAIRE. Sweetheart, I'm moving in with Aunt Nellie.

MARIE. The trailer?

CLAIRE. Yes.

MARIE. Why?

CLAIRE. Sweetheart, your father's leaving me.

MARIE. *He's* leaving *you*?

CLAIRE. He doesn't love me anymore.

MARIE. He's been fooling with other women for my whole lifetime and he's leaving you?

CLAIRE. No he hasn't Marie.

MARIE. You're so damn blind mother I can't stand it.

CLAIRE. The Lord will provide.

MARIE. Oh, Shut up!

CLAIRE. Marie!

MARIE. I'm tired of you. So sick and tired of you.

CLAIRE. He's leaving *me* and you're yelling at me?

MARIE. He left you a long time ago. Sally! Joanne! Marge! Claudia! I knew! You can't tell me that you didn't. Too blinded by the light mother? I'm tired of seeing you so ... so ... weak. Go! Live in your denial. Go! Live with the light. Go! Be your own embarrassment. I can't take it anymore! *(To abortion clinic.)* And I left.

DOCTOR. But you had something to tell her at your apartment, didn't you?

MARIE. I did. *(To MARIE's apartment.)* I'm not married.

CLAIRE. Oh, Marie, you didn't.

MARIE. No Mom, I didn't. I was … it's not important.

CLAIRE. You were what?

MARIE. Raped mother. I was raped. *(CLAIRE screams. She runs to MARIE, grabs her and hugs her with all her might. MARIE breaks down.)* Oh, mom. Oh, mom.

CLAIRE. What happened my baby? What happened?

MARIE. I was walking home. I was walking home. It was cold. I was walking home. And he came up from behind. It was late. Three thirty six A.M. Melissa's party. I was walking home and I felt cold metal nudged in my side and then a hand went over my face. I was walking home and he brought me into his apartment. I had no choice. I had no choice. His place was spotless. So clean. I looked up and it was him. It was the guy from the neighborhood. I saw him almost everyday. We said hi to each other. He was even handsome. All I wanted was to get back home. He told me things. Told me that he couldn't help himself. He kept apologizing. "I'm sorry, I'm sorry." I just wanted to get back home. I managed to let out one scream. One scream. There was something in its timbre. I heard it when I let it out. Like when daddy killed that deer. I sounded like that deer. All I wanted was to get back home. A neighbor heard. He had heard my deer scream. He called the police because he heard a tussle in the hallway also. All I wanted was to get back home. He finished. It was done. He said he was sorry. He kept apologizing. I just wanted to go home. He never let go of that gun. He never did. There was silence. He paced back and forth. The door got knocked down. It was the police. They saw he had a gun and they shot him. Killed him. They told me that he had a previous record and that's why they knocked the door down. They brought me to the hospital. But I just wanted to get back home.

CLAIRE. My baby. Oh, my baby.

MARIE. But I'm fine now. I am. I wouldn't keep the baby if he were still alive. I know that.

CLAIRE. I'm here for you. I love you sweetheart.

(To abortion clinic.)

MARIE. There's nothing like a mother's love.

DOCTOR. That's true, there isn't. You seem taken by that.

(Silence.)

MARIE. What? No. *(Holds her tummy.)* No. *(Pause.)* I'm not too proud about what I did next. We talked. For a while. Just about …

Nellie, the trailer, New York. But she seemed not to have changed. Not the way I wanted her to. So I set a little test for her. I wanted to see if she would speak her mind and commit to something, even if she is small-minded and bigoted, I wanted to hear something of some kind of anything come out of her mouth. So, I invited the men over without telling her of our plans. She didn't even know who they were. I wanted to see if she would say what she was thinking.... I knew that she was going to have a lot problems with it all. *(Knock on MARIE's apartment door.)* I threw my mom head first into my situation.... I stayed in the bathroom. *(To MARIE's apartment. Off stage.)* Oh, could you get that, Claire? It's them. I'll be right out.

    CLAIRE. Sure.... *(Under her breath.)* Claire.

(CLAIRE answers the door. MAX enters first.)

    MAX. Oh, hello?
    CLAIRE. Hello. Are you Marie's friend?

(Then STEVEN enters.)

    STEVEN. We are. Hi, I'm Steven. Marie told us that she had someone she wanted us to meet. I suppose you're her.

(Slight pause.)

    CLAIRE. Yes.
    MAX. I'm Max.
    CLAIRE. Hello, Max. It's nice to meet you.
    MAX. It's nice to meet you too.
    STEVEN. Where's Marie?
    CLAIRE. Bathroom.
    STEVEN. Oh.
    MAX. I'm sorry, but Marie didn't tell us who you were.
    CLAIRE. She didn't? Her mother. I'm her mother.
    STEVEN. Well, it is very nice to meet you.
    CLAIRE. Yes.

(Slight pause.)

    MAX. She's told us lots about you.
    CLAIRE. Oh, she has? What sort of things?
    MAX. Um, Ohio!
    STEVEN. *(Immediately, as if to save MAX.)* You're from Ohio, right?
    CLAIRE. Yes.

(Slight pause.)

MAX. I'm from nearby Pennsylvania. I lived by the border. We used to go to Ohio often.

CLAIRE. I hardly ever make it to Pennsylvania. They have nice trees though.

STEVEN. Oh, you're into horticulture?

CLAIRE. No.

(Slight pause.)

STEVEN. Oh, well, I like trees myself. The leaves. Those are what I ....

CLAIRE. *(Interrupting.)* I'm sure Marie will be right out.

STEVEN. Right.

(MARIE comes out of the bathroom.)

MARIE. Hello sweetcakes...es. I see you've met my mother.

STEVEN. We did.

MAX. I didn't know your mom was supposed to come for a visit.

MARIE. She wasn't. She sent one of her spies who saw us at F.A.O. Schwarz. My aunt Nellie. She followed me home and called my mother to tell her where I lived.

CLAIRE. Spies ... really, Marie. Nellie wanted to talk to you so badly, but she thought it would be better if I spoke to you alone.

MARIE. Nellie told my mother that I was pregnant.

CLAIRE. That's when I decided to come.

MARIE. You wouldn't have come if I weren't pregnant?

CLAIRE. Oh, Marie ....

MARIE. Would you have, mother?

CLAIRE. Of course.

STEVEN. Marie, I hope you are taking good care of yourself.

MARIE. Of course I am. I wouldn't let anything happen to our baby.

MAX. Steven and I just came from looking at cribs at Macy's.

MARIE. We can go to Toy's R Us. I'm sure they're cheaper.

MAX. But not as nice.

MARIE. But cheaper.

MAX. Well, your crib can be from Toy's R Us and ours will be from Macy's. No big deal.

MARIE. I think the baby should have the same crib in both places, don't you?

STEVEN. That might be a good idea, Max.

MAX. I don't see why.

STEVEN. Claire, so much planning is involved when you're

expecting a baby. How did you ever do it?

CLAIRE. I don't remember.

STEVEN. Yes, I suppose this is nothing. Just wait until we actually have the kid.

MARIE. I know, it'll be crazy.

CLAIRE. I'm confused.

MARIE. About what?

CLAIRE. Oh, did I say that? Excuse me.

MARIE. What is it mother?

CLAIRE. Please Marie, just let it be.

STEVEN. What's for dinner?

MARIE. I was thinking pizza.

MAX. You've been thinking pizza for the last three weeks.

MARIE. I can't get enough of it.

MAX. You should have seen it, Claire. Last week the three of us ordered in pizza and these two ganged up on me. They wanted ....

MARIE and STEVEN. Anchovies!

MAX. Uch! Steven, I'm still contemplating disowning you for your taste in food.

STEVEN. I'm sorry, baby. Come here. Incentive for not disowning me ....

(STEVEN kisses MAX. MARIE smiles at CLAIRE.)

MARIE. Fine. Pepperoni.

MAX. Doesn't your mother have any say?

MARIE. Mom? *(Beat.)* No ... she has no say.

MAX. Great! Then pepperoni it is.

CLAIRE. I need to go for a walk. I'll be back.

STEVEN. I'll go with you.

CLAIRE. No! I'll be fine. I exercise before fattening food. I'll go it alone. This way I can keep my own pace.

MARIE. It's Ok. Let her go. The pizza will be here in a half hour. Don't be long.

(CLAIRE leaves; to abortion clinic.)

MARIE. And that was the introduction. It was mean, I know and I'm sorry. Well, the night was more of the same. Talking about nonsense. The look on my mother's face said it all. She didn't approve that I was planning to raise my child with an interracial homosexual couple. But what did I care? Oh, by the way, she didn't go for a walk. I'm sure of it. She had to find some way to stay. And she did. It was the next morning. She was leaving when...

(To MARIE's apartment.)

CLAIRE. It's gone!

MARIE. What?

CLAIRE. Nellie's car. It's gone! It's gone!

MARIE. Where did you park?

CLAIRE. *(Points out window.)* There.

MARIE. I never saw a car there.

CLAIRE. It was there. I swear. Right across the street.

MARIE. Claire, that's a no parking zone.

CLAIRE. A what?

MARIE. A no park … oh, forget it.

CLAIRE. Well, where did they take the car?

MARIE. It's a three-day weekend, Claire. You can't just get it back. It's New York.

CLAIRE. What do I do?

MARIE. You stay. That's what you do. You have no choice.

CLAIRE. Thank you sweetie. I hate to be a bother ….

MARIE. There's no room here, mother. But Max and Steven have an extra bedroom. You can sleep there. I'm sure they won't mind.

CLAIRE. No. That's fine. I'll find a motel.

MARIE. Claire, you don't want to stay in one of the cheap motels here in the city. Trust me, you don't. Why can't you just stay with Max and Steven?

CLAIRE. Because ….

MARIE. Why?

CLAIRE. Because I don't … I …. Please. Let me stay on your couch again. I don't mind.

MARIE. *(Pause.)* Fine. *(To abortion clinic.)* And that's when the tug-of-war began.

(To MARIE's apartment.)

CLAIRE. I found some hot chocolate.

MARIE. Where did you find that? I haven't bought hot chocolate in years.

CLAIRE. No matter, it's those powder mixes. I'm sure it's fine. Isn't it the powdered stuff that they drink in space?

MARIE. I think.

CLAIRE. Then it's fine. Here. *(She hands MARIE a cup of hot chocolate.)* The guys, they're nice.

MARIE. *(A little surprised.)* You think?

CLAIRE. I do. Where do you know them from, again?

MARIE. Ginsberg, Ginsberg, Blindman and Ginsberg. I was a temp for Max.

CLAIRE. Ah. They seem very caring.

MARIE. They are. So, you don't mind ….

CLAIRE. Mind?

MARIE. That they're together?

CLAIRE. "Thou shalt not judge."

MARIE. Of course.

CLAIRE. I remember making hot chocolate for you when you were a kid. You loved it. *(Starts stroking MARIE's hair.)* May I?

MARIE. Sure.

CLAIRE. There was this one night when your father was coming home late and you got worried about where he was. He was working late, that was all, but you got so worried. Your bottom lip was trembling because you thought he was gone forever. You know how kids are. Getting worried at the slightest thing. I tried to calm you by making some hot chocolate. You cried and cried and cried. You know how kids imaginations run away from them. You thought the world was ending. Kids just don't understand how things work. If things aren't the way things should be, they lash out. They get upset.

MARIE. And how should things be?

CLAIRE. Normal.

MARIE. Right. *(Moves away from the stroking.)* Are you sure you're all right with the guys?

CLAIRE. Why would you ask that? I said I'm fine. I feel foolish about the car.

MARIE. Don't worry about it. *(Beat.)* The hair thing felt good ....

(CLAIRE strokes MARIE's hair again.)

CLAIRE. I'm just not used to driving.

MARIE. You have to read the signs, is all.

CLAIRE. You never said that it was good to see me.

MARIE. No, I didn't.

CLAIRE. Is it?

MARIE. I'm confused.

CLAIRE. We're all confused. This is life.

MARIE. The world *is* rather crazy.

CLAIRE. I think it's New York that's crazy.

MARIE. True. Very true.

CLAIRE. Do you want to stay here forever?

MARIE. I don't think so.

CLAIRE. Where would you go?

MARIE. I don't know. Someplace warm.

CLAIRE. Max and Steven would go with you?

MARIE. Don't know. Never asked them.

CLAIRE. Hmm. *(Beat.)* Does this mean I'm back in your life?

MARIE. You're here, right?

CLAIRE. Yes. Where do the guys live?

MARIE. Brooklyn.

CLAIRE. Sounds far away.

MARIE. Not really.

CLAIRE. I think the baby should have the same crib in both places.

MARIE. Me too. I'm not sure what Max was thinking.

CLAIRE. The best thing would be if the baby had only one crib.

MARIE. Probably. But that's not possible. I don't have the resources to do it alone.

CLAIRE. You don't have to do it alone.

MARIE. No, I have Max and Steven. They've wanted a child for so long. They've been turned away from so many opportunities.

CLAIRE. I wonder why.

MARIE. Look at them and their lifestyle. That's why.

CLAIRE. You see it too?

MARIE. *(Pulling away from CLAIRE's stroking.)* See what?

CLAIRE. That life is going to be difficult. Logistics. You have to think about logistics.

MARIE. I know.

CLAIRE. *(Starts to stroke MARIE's hair again.)* My baby. I love you.

MARIE. I ... I'm glad you came. *(To abortion clinic.)* Score one for my mother. But she got me thinking .... *(to MAX and STEVEN's house.)* I had to come over.

STEVEN. It's fine. What is it?

MARIE. We have to think about what we're doing.

MAX. Where's your mom?

MARIE. Home. She's scared of the subways. Even with me.

MAX. So what do you mean?

MARIE. I mean, what? ... We're really going to have this baby going from place to place every two weeks?

STEVEN. I guess.

MARIE. We can't guess. We have to know.

STEVEN. So yes, we'll devise a schedule.

MARIE. It's scientific then. So sterile.

STEVEN. How do you want to do it? You could move in here I suppose.

MARIE. But the other room will be the baby's. And I can't live here. I want my own life.

MAX. You'll have your own life.

MARIE. I will not be taken in like charity. I was raped. I'm not a child.

MAX. Ok, Marie. Look, you decided to keep this baby. We decided to raise it as a family. All these matters, we can work them out.

MARIE. I know. I think. Will you guys move to Florida with me?

STEVEN. Florida?

MAX. Maybe.

STEVEN. No.

MARIE. Just wanted constant warmth, that's all. It's going to get cold here again, in a few months. I just wanted some warmth. *(Exhales.)* It's Ok. It's Ok. I'll stay here. That's fine.

STEVEN. I think we can use our famous three-way hug, don't you?

MARIE. I think so, yes.

(They do their famous three-way hug.)

MAX. We're going to do this. Logistical problems or no, we'll do this.

(To abortion clinic.)

DOCTOR. The three of them. They're pulling you.

MARIE. Yes. They are. The next day, Sunday, got worse. Deep down, I was happy my mom was there. I guess I let that get in the way of my plans.

(To MARIE's apartment.)

CLAIRE. It's nice to spend this time with you.

MARIE. It is. If it seemed as if I wasn't happy to see you at first, I'm happy now.

CLAIRE. And I'm happy too, sweetheart. Can we play ....

MARIE. Rummy?

CLAIRE. I brought our deck.

(CLAIRE pulls out a worn deck of cards.)

MARIE. Our cards?

CLAIRE. I was hoping we could play together.

MARIE. *(Takes the deck in her hands.)* I'd love to play.

CLAIRE. Then get dealing.

(MARIE starts to shuffle and then deals the cards. A game ensues.)

MARIE. These cards. I remember being what? four? five? when we started playing.

CLAIRE. You were young.

MARIE. Do you miss dad?

CLAIRE. Yes I do. I miss him greatly.

MARIE. You do realize he's a shmuck. He was having affairs ever since I can remember playing with these cards.

CLAIRE. I ... I ....

MARIE. Mom. Please. Acknowledge it.

CLAIRE. But ... I ... I ... still love him.

MARIE. All right. I don't understand but all right.

CLAIRE. The Lord works in mysterious ways, Marie.

MARIE. Please, for the sake of our new start together don't say that to me again.

CLAIRE. Fine. He hurt you didn't he?

MARIE. He did. And even if you don't want to admit it, he hurt you too.

CLAIRE. He hurt me by making you turn against me.

MARIE. I couldn't stand it mother. I couldn't stand by and watch you be so ....

CLAIRE. I believe the word you used was weak.

MARIE. Yes. I couldn't stay and watch you be so weak.

CLAIRE. And what's different now?

MARIE. I'm older.

CLAIRE. *(Exhales.)* Yes. We all are. *(Pause while game playing.)* Marie, what about your father and I made you so horribly angry?

MARIE. I wanted a real mother and father.

CLAIRE. Oh?

MARIE. I wanted a father who took care of me and I wanted a mother who didn't live in denial. I suppose I just wanted everything to be ... to be ....

CLAIRE. What?

MARIE. Normal.

CLAIRE. You shouldn't be ashamed of that. Normalcy is what we all want.

MARIE. What am I doing?

CLAIRE. With the guys?

MARIE. With it all.

CLAIRE. I don't know.

MARIE. Mom, I don't know either.

CLAIRE. Come. Come back with me.

MARIE. I can't.

CLAIRE. Please. We'll pick up again. I'll move from Nellie's and with the two of us, we can get a new place.

MARIE. The guys.

CLAIRE. They'll live.

MARIE. I don't know.

CLAIRE. We can do it. Think about it.

MARIE. Oh God. Oh God.

CLAIRE. What is it?

MARIE. I need to nap. *(Lays her cards on the table.)* There, I forfeit. You win. *(Walks in the direction of the bedroom; then to abortion clinic.)* And she did win. She's a mastermind. She got me to say exactly what she wanted me to. That I wanted normalcy. She knew what she was doing. Those damn cards, talking about my father. Everything.

DOCTOR. You could take it that way, yes.

MARIE. It becomes a hell of a lot clearer. That night I went over to Max and Steven's. *(That night. At guys' apartment. MAX and STEVEN enter.)* We need to talk.

MAX. What is it, baby?

MARIE. This is hard.

STEVEN. What is it?

MARIE. I've been thinking.

STEVEN. Yes?

MARIE. Have we thought about this clearly?

MAX. Don't you do this.

MARIE. If you'd only think about things.

STEVEN. It's your mother. Isn't it?

MARIE. No.

STEVEN. You can't do this. We've been planning.

MARIE. I know.

MAX. What's the problem?

MARIE. Normalcy.

MAX. What about it?

MARIE. I want it.

STEVEN. Are we abnormal?

MARIE. No. That's not what I mean.

STEVEN. It sounds like it.

MARIE. I want don't want this baby to be maladjusted when it grows up.

STEVEN. It won't be.

MARIE. I am.

MAX. Who isn't?

MARIE. I always wanted a real family. We wouldn't be one.

MAX. We will be. We'll be whatever we want to be.

MARIE. Stop giving me that general shit and give me something concrete.

STEVEN. You want concrete? Fine. You can't give the financial opportunities that this baby deserves the same way that we can. Financially, we'll help. When you want to start dating, having boyfriends you are going to need some free time. We'll help with that. When this baby starts asking about his biological father, we'll help with that. We'll be the male influences this baby needs. We'll support you when you're tired. We'll be the reason that the baby will be unprejudiced and open. Don't take this way from us. We'll be the family that this baby needs.

MARIE. I know you'd be. Oh jeez, I need some time.

MAX. This is her isn't it? She asked you to go back with her.

MARIE. Yes but ... it's me.

MAX. We're coming over. The four of us are going to talk. Come on.

MARIE. Not now. Let's sleep on it. Let's talk with a clear head. Tomorrow.

STEVEN. We'll be there at eleven.

MARIE. Don't attack her. She's had enough of that.

MAX. We'll see you at eleven.

MARIE. Guys, I want you as fathers. I do.

MAX. Then what's the problem?

MARIE. It's that ... I ... I ... *(Starts to cry.)* I need some sleep.

STEVEN. Stay here. Sleep here.

MARIE. I can't leave her alone. I already did that once. Tomorrow. We'll talk tomorrow. *(Starts on her way out.)* Can we have our famous three-way hug? *(They do their famous three-way hug. Light change, to abortion clinic.)* And that was the last time we ever hugged.

DOCTOR. Is it now Monday?

MARIE. Yes. Labor Day.

DOCTOR. Three days ago.

MARIE. When I ran away. *(To MARIE's apartment, knock on door.)* Who is it?

STEVEN. It's us. *(MARIE opens the door. The guys enter. Simultaneously, CLAIRE enters from the direction of the suggested bedroom.)* Claire.

CLAIRE. Steven. Max.

MAX. Claire.

CLAIRE. I asked Marie to come home with me.

MAX. She's not going to.

CLAIRE. Don't push me. She's going to.

MAX. *(To MARIE.)* And that's what you want?

CLAIRE. Of course.

STEVEN. Do we have any say in this?

CLAIRE. I don't think so.

STEVEN. That's not true.

CLAIRE. You're pushing.... I think the two of you are taking advantage of my baby's bad situation.

MAX. *(Exploding.)* Us? You!

CLAIRE. Me? She's my daughter.

STEVEN. So?

MAX. Stop! We shouldn't be arguing.

CLAIRE. You're right. So let's not argue. I have a question for you.

MAX. Yes?

CLAIRE. What if the baby turns out to be a boy?

STEVEN. What is that supposed to mean?

CLAIRE. Just answer.

STEVEN. Then we'll molest him everyday.

CLAIRE. That's it. That's too much. You've pushed.

MAX. Steven, stop it.

STEVEN. That's what she was alluding to.

CLAIRE. I was not.

MAX. Look, we might be two men but we have just as much of a right as anybody else to raise a child in the world.

CLAIRE. How much do you want to be like everybody else?

MAX. What do you mean?

CLAIRE. I mean, Marie's told me that you've been trying to become fathers for some time.

MAX. Yes.

CLAIRE. Why do you think you've been turned away so many times? Because you aren't like everyone else.

STEVEN. We aren't?

CLAIRE. You are two men trying to pass as being a normal couple. Only in New York.

STEVEN. I pray for you.

CLAIRE. You pray for me?

STEVEN. To open your eyes.

CLAIRE. We'll be using the same prayer then.

MAX. Look, we've known Marie for almost ten years, ever since she came to New York. It's not like we're waltzing in to try to take her away. She made her choice to live here in New York. Away from you.

CLAIRE. That was because I was weak. Right, Marie? Well, I can't be like that anymore.

STEVEN. Where will you live? In the trailer?

CLAIRE. We'll find a place.

STEVEN. We can give more. We can provide a financially stable environment for the child.

CLAIRE. Money isn't everything.

STEVEN. Neither is therapy.

CLAIRE. What?

STEVEN. You're using the baby as a chance to try again with Marie. Why didn't you come earlier?

CLAIRE. She didn't want to see me.

STEVEN. I would have found her nine years and three hundred sixty four days ago if I truly loved her. I wouldn't have waited ten years and for the news that she was pregnant.

CLAIRE. I want this baby!

STEVEN. You failed the first time and you want to try again.

CLAIRE. You shut up! What do you know? You know nothing.

STEVEN. It seems like I do.

CLAIRE. You have no right to come in the middle of my family.

STEVEN. You failed the first time. What makes you think you won't do it again?

CLAIRE. I'm not listening to a nigger faggot about how to run my life! *(Gasps.)* Oh my! I'm sorry. I didn't say that.

MAX. You claim to have the light of the Lord ....

CLAIRE. I do! It's you that is devoid of that.

MAX. I don't need it nor do I want it.

CLAIRE. Marie, I need that child. I've spent the last ten years thinking about what I've done wrong. About what I could do over again. I messed up with your daddy. I don't know how I did but I did. Maybe I could have slept with him more, but that's dir... no, Oh God! What am I saying? I messed up with you. Without even knowing that I did, I did. Maybe I could have taken some action against him but I couldn't. I was scared. I was alone. I was weak. But I'm ready to try again. I've lost you and your father already. Let me just have the baby. I can't die knowing that these two are raising the child that I should be holding in my arms every day. I can't die knowing that you picked these two just to hurt me. I can't die knowing that I'm still the reason you make these awful decisions. I can't die like that.

MAX. Wait, can't we all be a part of the baby's life?

STEVEN. Max! I'm not sharing anything with someone who spits venom out at me.

MAX. She was upset.

STEVEN. She hurt me.

CLAIRE. Yes ... yes ... what a good idea. I'm sorry Steven. Let's all be the family. Let's all be a family.

STEVEN. I don't think you're a suitable role model for our child.

CLAIRE. It's not your child.

STEVEN. Nor is it yours.

CLAIRE. I worked too hard for this. I spent the weekend here! I've had enough. I'M YOUR MOTHER! PACK YOUR BAGS MARIE! I'M YOUR MOTHER!

(MARIE starts to go towards her bedroom.)

MAX. *(To MARIE.)* YOU STUPID BITCH! IT'S OURS!

(Pause.)

STEVEN. He means something else.

CLAIRE. No he doesn't.

STEVEN. He meant something different.

MAX. I did.

CLAIRE. True colors?

STEVEN. No.

CLAIRE. Marie, pack your bags.

STEVEN. Marie, no! You can't. This is our last chance. No one's going to come through for us. You walk out that door; you'll be killing our dreams. We were so close. This was our blessing. Please, don't do it.

CLAIRE. Her rape was your blessing?

MAX. It was yours too.

CLAIRE. It was my chance.

MARIE. You're animals.

CLAIRE. No.

MAX. We're not.

MARIE. I can't raise the child with any of you.

CLAIRE. But I spoke up. I spoke my mind. That's what you wanted ....

MARIE. It was ugly.

MAX. We aren't.

MARIE. You are.

STEVEN. *(Stepping away from MAX.)* I'm not.

MARIE. You're so desperate.

STEVEN. But ....

MARIE. I can't bring this child into the world like this. It's an ugly place. It's cold and lonely. And all of you just make it lonelier. Look at you, talking about me as if I'm a rag doll that can be thrown around. And my child! None of you love my child. Mom, you can't try again. You failed the first time. My child is not an experiment. Max, Steven, you didn't want to help me or this child. It could have been any child. You just want to prove that you can be like everybody else.

STEVEN. No!

MARIE. Yes! You all want to do what you will with me. I can't take it anymore. I'm tired. I don't want to be raped anymore. It's my life.

CLAIRE. Marie ....

MARIE. I'm leaving.

CLAIRE. Not again!

MARIE. *(Holding her belly.)* I'm ending it.

STEVEN. No!

MARIE. I love this child too much to bring it into this world.

CLAIRE. You can't. You'll go to Hell!

MARIE. I'm leaving.

STEVEN. But your apartment.

MARIE. Not a problem.

MAX. But ....

MARIE. Goodbye. *(MARIE leaves the apartment. MAX, STEVEN and CLAIRE are left alone. Lights down. Momentary blackout. Lights up again on MARIE on chair with DOCTOR standing over her, just as it was at the beginning.)* And that's what happened.

DOCTOR. You boarded a bus?

MARIE. Yep. It didn't matter which one. Just that it took me far away.

DOCTOR. So you're here.

MARIE. I am.

DOCTOR. So. What do you want to do?

MARIE. *(Pause.)* I ... I want to do it.

DOCTOR. All right. I see, you've read all the materials. Then let's get started. I'll be right back ....

(The DOCTOR leaves the room. MARIE is left alone for what should seem like a while. She is sitting alone on the chair.)

DOCTOR. All right, Marie.

MARIE. No! I want to do it.

DOCTOR. Do it?

MARIE. It's my choice and I want to keep it.

DOCTOR. Oh, I see.

MARIE. The world *is* ugly but ....

DOCTOR. Back to New York?

MARIE. Definitely not.

DOCTOR. Where then?

MARIE. I don't know. Someplace warm.

(MARIE gets up and leaves the clinic. The DOCTOR looks after her. He then opens the door to the waiting room.)

DOCTOR. Next!

(Blackout.)

END OF THE PLAY

SET DESCRIPTION

Considering the swift location changes in the play and the playwright's penchant for theatricality, it is important to remember that the play needn't be bogged down with a realistic set. *Someplace Warm* was originally produced using only eight chairs and a desk for the doctor. The chairs were moved into different configurations in order to create the various settings indicated in the script. Since the entire play essentially takes place in the abortion clinic and the characters are living in Marie's mind as she recounts her story, the actors were free to seamlessly move the chairs into the different configurations as they moved from one scene to the next. A similar approach is recommended.

PROPERTIES

3 wine glasses
2 hot chocolate mugs
1 McDonald's bag filled with toys
1 worn deck of cards
1 clipboard
1 stethoscope
Crossword puzzle *(optional for MAX in the first scene in his and Steven's apartment)*

COSTUME LIST

Contemporary casual clothes appropriate to each character (i.e. a long floral dress for CLARE with a cross around her neck, jeans and a T-shirt for MARIE, etc.)

THE TEST

by

Paula J. Caplan

*With respect and appreciation to
Billy Neal Moore — "Cleveland" — for letting us tell his story,
and to Richard Lay and Shannon Sweeney
and all the folks at Sage Theatre Company*

THE TEST was presented in New York by Richard Lay and Sage Theatre Company in August 2001 at the Chernuchin Theatre at 314 West 54th Street. It was directed by Paula J. Caplan, who also did the scene and costume design, with the following cast:

BRADLEY...Keith Mascoll
CLEVELAND...Ricardo Pitts-Wiley

THE TEST had its West Coast premiere produced by Playwrights' Circle at the Black Box Theatre in Palm Springs, California, in November, 2001 under the direction of Rod Roeser. Lighting design was by Ron Brian and Eric Bolton. The cast was as follows:

BRADLEY...Dan Graff
CLEVELAND..Sam Hankerson

ABOUT THE AUTHOR

PAULA J. CAPLAN is the author of *CALL ME CRAZY*, which won awards from the Arlene and William Lewis National playwriting Contest for Women and the Rhode Island State Council of the Arts, as well as a Sage Best New Play nomination. Other plays produced by Sage Theatre company include *LOVE'S HOLLOW* and *TIKKUN OLAM: REPAIRING THE WORLD*. Her stage writing has been performed across the United States, from Palm Springs to Fort Worth to New York and Boston. She is also an actor, director and producer.

CHARACTERS

BRADLEY: A Black male in his mid-twenties
CLEVELAND: A Black male in his mid-twenties or older

SETTING

Place: Scene 1   Death Row
       Scene 2   The same, two days later

Time: The Present

Scene 1

(CLEVELAND and BRADLEY are onstage, seated. BRADLEY holds a Bible and is reading from it. When reading, BRADLEY is slow and takes frequent pauses to work it out.)

BRADLEY. Yuh ... eeee. *(Beat.)* Yuh-ee, yee!

CLEVELAND. Close.

BRADLEY. Not yee?

CLEVELAND. Why do you say it's yee?

BRADLEY. It starts with "y," and then there's "e" "a," and you said "e" "a" sounds like "ee" like in "eat."

CLEVELAND. You know, you're right. That's good. But sometimes "e" "a" sounds like "ay."

BRADLEY. Not another one. Why can't a rule ever be a rule? Why is there always "but sometimes the rule's no good"?

CLEVELAND. That's just how it is. I know it's hard.

BRADLEY. So this is ....

CLEVELAND. It's "yay." Go on.

BRADLEY. *(Reading, pronouncing "Yea" correctly.)* "Yea ... thog. Yea, thog ...."

CLEVELAND. This "g" is silent, and so is the "h."

BRADLEY. "Yea, thou"?

CLEVELAND. Well, that's a good Bible word, but this one is "though. Yea, though." Go on.

BRADLEY. "Yea, though I walk" — it's walk, isn't it! *(Beat.)* "throw ..."

CLEVELAND. "through. I walk through ..."

BRADLEY. "through the ... val-ley of the sha ... um ... sha-dow, shadow! ... of ... um, daith"? It's "e" then "a" like "yea," so daith?

CLEVELAND. It's "death." You sure chose a hard psalm.

BRADLEY. Yes, but ....

CLEVELAND. I know. I know. *(Beat.)* Hey, don't feel bad, man. I can't believe how far you've come. Words like "Adam" and "Eve" and "Eden" and even "snake" are lots easier than these. Six months ago you couldn't do those, and now you breeze right through them. This stuff today is really, really difficult. Want to take a short break?

BRADLEY. OK. *(Beat.)* I don't know why you help me so much.

CLEVELAND. I'll help anyone who wants that much to learn. 'Specially this book. That's my thing in here, Bradley. My whole purpose is to help guys who want to read better. And read this better.

BRADLEY. It's not stupid to try to learn now?

CLEVELAND. Any more than me trying to teach now?

BRADLEY. You got me there. We'll both be dead before Easter.

CLEVELAND. You might not. Not with your new one.

BRADLEY. Man, she's a fighter, ain't she? She was here this morning.

CLEVELAND. Any news?

BRADLEY. Um, yeah, I forgot to tell you. The judge says I've got to get the test.

CLEVELAND. *The* test? No joke?

BRADLEY. Right. A psy-chiatrist is coming tomorrow to give it to me.

CLEVELAND. I think it's a psychologist who gives that kind of test.

BRADLEY. What's the difference?

CLEVELAND. *(Answering the question but actually focusing on the news.)* Psychiatrists are shrink doctors. Psychologists are called "Dr. Something" but they're not doctor-doctors. They do the tests to see how smart you are.

BRADLEY. They want to see if I'm dumb enough they should fry me?

CLEVELAND. No, Bradley. They didn't tell you?

BRADLEY. Tell me what?

CLEVELAND. The test is because if you're *not* smart they *can't* electrocute you.

BRADLEY. Why not? I killed the guy.

CLEVELAND. Yes, but you thought he was hurting your mother.

BRADLEY. Yes, I did. And I thought she was yelling because she wanted him to stop. And everybody said I was a dumb-ass 'cause I didn't know.

CLEVELAND. I know. So now you've finally got a lawyer who really listened. And she believes you. See, Bradley, lots of guys woulda known that wasn't why your ma was yelling. And Ms. Jules told the judge she can prove you didn't understand. You really thought you were helping your mother. The test will show that you didn't hurt him for a *mean* reason. And then the law says they can't kill you.

BRADLEY. She said something about they can't, but she's so nice I just thought she didn't want me to feel sad.

CLEVELAND. No, she was telling the truth. Bradley, this is wonderful!

BRADLEY. So the test is they'll ask why I killed that guy? I'll get to say I didn't mean to be mean?

CLEVELAND. No. The test is to find out how smart you are.

BRADLEY. *(Sad.)* Aw, no! No way I can pass that test.

CLEVELAND. *(Not noticing BRADLEY is sad.)* Whoa, there *is* a

God! And He is good!

BRADLEY. They always put me in the dumbest group. In fifth grade I was the only one in "Spiders" group for reading. No way I can pass.

CLEVELAND. *(Realizing BRADLEY doesn't get it.)* Bradley, listen to me. You don't *want* to pass this test. This is the one time it's *good* to flunk a test. Good? Hey, it's great!

BRADLEY. It's *good* to flunk?!

CLEVELAND. Listen to me, Bradley. Your reading has gotten so much better.

BRADLEY. Thanks to you, my man!

CLEVELAND. But listen. That means it will be easier for you to read the questions on the test and know some right answers.

BRADLEY. Yeah!

CLEVELAND. So you can be sure to give *wrong* answers.

BRADLEY. Give wrong answers?

CLEVELAND. Yes, Bradley. You *need* to flunk.

BRADLEY. I *need* to flunk?

CLEVELAND. Yes. For this test, it is good to flunk.

BRADLEY. Good to flunk??! Hallelujah!

CLEVELAND. Hallelujah, baby!

(They dance gloriously.)

CLEVELAND. Man, if they tested you for dancing, you'd be at the top of the class!

BRADLEY. Yeah, music was the good part of school. *(Rapping and dancing, first makes rap rhythm sounds with no words, then begins with the words.)* Yo, bro', didja hear, didja hear about the test?

CLEVELAND. *(Joining the dancing and rapping.)* No, man, I never heard, never heard about the test.

BRADLEY. It's the test, it's the test where the worst is the best!

CLEVELAND. It's the test, it's the test where the worst is the best!

(They make more rap rhythm sounds with no words, then resume the words.)

BRADLEY. I'd never thunk that it's *good* to flunk!

CLEVELAND. You'd never thunk that it's good to flunk?

BRADLEY. And if I fail,

CLEVELAND. And if you fail ...

BRADLEY. I'll get *out* of jail! I'll get *out* of jail!

(BRADLEY goes on alone with rap rhythm sounds and goes on dancing alone, but CLEVELAND stops.)

CLEVELAND. Brad, my man, wait. You gotta know this. If you fail the test, you won't die in the chair, but they might not let you out. It just depends.

BRADLEY. Oh. Yeah. Depends on the judge?

CLEVELAND. I don't know for sure. Maybe a judge. Maybe another jury trial. Ask Ms. Jules.

(Silence.)

BRADLEY. But wait! Hey, that's OK! Just me not dyin' would mean so much to Ma. *(Beat.)* And, then, if I know I'm gonna live, I can do a lot of stuff in *here. (Beat.)* I'll get me a band together!

CLEVELAND. That'd be great. Bradley, it's gonna happen. I know it. It's gonna happen.

(A celebratory hand clasp between them.)

BRADLEY. But. Aw, no. But you … I mean … even if I get off, there ain't gonna be a test for you, right? Cause they know you'd never flunk.

CLEVELAND. Right. But this minute, Bradley, I'm so happy for you I don't care about me. I've known for a long time there was no way out for me.

BRADLEY. Hold on! That's what I thought about me. But look now! I know, I'll talk to Ms. Jules about you. She's so damn smart I know she can think of something.

CLEVELAND. You're a good man, Bradley. Thank you. But it doesn't really matter. See, the guy I killed, it wasn't like with your Ma. I killed him because I thought no one was home when I went to rob his house, and suddenly he was there with a gun. And, well, I had a gun because … I always had one. And I've always been hotheaded.

BRADLEY. Your head is hot?

CLEVELAND. Huh? Oh, not really hot. It means it's real easy to get me mad. Bradley, when I killed that guy, I wasn't trying to help anyone. I knew *exactly* what I was doing. It's taken me fifteen years, but I've found the Lord, and I'm ready to go. I've made my peace with God. All I want is to know you're going to live. No foolin'. Because you weren't out for yourself. You never meant to hurt anybody.

BRADLEY. But Cleve, I shoulda known. I shoulda known. If I hadn't been so stupid I would've. It ain't like I didn't know about … I mean, *I'd* even … it's just, I'd never seen Ma like that. And she'd always helped me, told me I didn't need to be smart, just try my best.

CLEVELAND. It's good that she did that, Bradley.

BRADLEY. Yeah, she said as long as I tried hard, I shouldn't worry about smart or dumb. That made me feel better. And I never got to do nothin' to help her. So when I saw ... it didn't get into my dumb head what it was. Stupid. My whole damn life. Stupid.

CLEVELAND. Bradley, the guard's coming. Give 'em hell tomorrow. Hey, maybe this is the one test you can enjoy! Huh?

(They slap hands. BRADLEY exits. Change lighting in some way that indicates passage of time but does not suggest that the play is over; going to a special on CLEVELAND may work. As BRADLEY exits, CLEVELAND keeps moving, such as watching BRADLEY leave, then going back to the table, sitting down, picking up and looking at the Bible, all the while repeating some of the rhyming he and BRADLEY were just doing.)

Scene 2

(Two days have passed. Lights come fully up on CLEVELAND as BRADLEY enters.)

CLEVELAND. My man!

(CLEVELAND stands and goes to slap hands with BRADLEY, but BRADLEY doesn't respond to him and goes over, sits in CLEVELAND's chair, picks up the Bible, and makes an exaggerated show of putting his feet on the other chair and paging through the Bible as though he is easily reading it.)

BRADLEY. Cleve.
CLEVELAND. So. *(Beat.)* You had the test?
BRADLEY. Yes.
CLEVELAND. Bradley, you're killing me! Did they say how you did?
BRADLEY. Yeah, Cleve.
CLEVELAND. That smile! That smile! You flunked! Oh Bradley, my man, free at last, you're free at last!

(CLEVELAND starts to dance.)

BRADLEY. Cleve. I ... um ... I passed.
CLEVELAND. As in flunked. Passed because you flunked. Right? They can't fry you now, right?
BRADLEY. Passed because I passed. Seventy is passing, and I got more than that. I got 71!
CLEVELAND. *(Beat.)* Oh, no! Oh, Brad, didn't I explain it right? I thought you understood!

BRADLEY. Cleveland, you did right. I understood.

CLEVELAND. Then what happened?

BRADLEY. Nobody ever believed it, but I always did try my best. Cleveland, I tried so hard. And I did it. I finally did it. Be happy for me, Cleveland. It's the only test I ever passed.

(Blackout.)

END OF THE PLAY

SET DESCRIPTION

One table (card table size, institutional looking)
Two chairs (institutional looking)

(Table and chairs are far downstage but far enough up to allow the actors to cross in front of them.)

PROPERTIES

A Bible

COSTUMES

White T-shirts
Jeans
Socks, and sneakers

or

Death Row prisoners' uniforms

(No belts or shoelaces, because not allowed on Death Row)

.

A CLOSER LOOK

by

Arlene Hutton

For Donna Lincks
With love and thanks for all her support

A CLOSER LOOK premiered at Vital Theatre Company, 432 West 42ᴺᴰ Street, New York City, Stephen Sunderlin, Artistic Director, (as part of Women@Work), in June, 2002, directed by Sharon Fallon. The costume design was by Shelley Norton, the lighting design was by Aaron Spivey, the set design was by Todd Buttera, the sound design was by Alf Bishai and the stage manager was Fran Rubenstein. The cast was as follows:

DENISE..Lynne Halliday
LAINIE...Irene McDonnell
TISH..Carol Halstead
AMANDA...Melissa Rayworth
BOBBI...Veronica M. Kehoe

A CLOSER LOOK was presented by Vital Theatre Company for the Samuel French Festival on August 12, 2002. It was directed by Sharon Fallon, the costume design was by Shelley Norton, the lighting design was by Aaron Spivey, the set design was by Todd Buttera, the sound design was by Alf Bishai and the stage manager was Fran Rubenstein. The cast was as follows:

DENISE..Lynne Halliday
LAINIE...Irene McDonnell
TISH..Carol Halstead
AMANDA..Stephanie Cozart
BOBBI...Veronica M. Kehoe

ABOUT THE AUTHOR

ARLENE HUTTON is a member of New Dramatists. She is the author of *LAST TRAIN TO NIBROC* (New York Drama League nomination for Best Play 2000), *AS IT IS IN HEAVEN* and *I DREAM BEFORE I TAKE THE STAND*. Two of her one-act plays, *STUDIO PORTRAIT* and *THE PRICE YOU PAY* are previous Sam French Short Play Festival winners. *PUSHING BUTTONS* and *CUBICLES* were finalists for the Heineman Award at Actors' Theatre of Louisville. Her plays have been performed in New York City, across the country and abroad.

CHARACTERS

DENISE: a hairdresser, probably still in her thirties
LAINIE: a dresser, probably forty
TISH: a talk show host, won't tell her age
AMANDA: a segment producer, definitely under thirty
BOBBI: a make-up artist, fifties.

SETTING

Place: Tish's dressing room in the studio where her talk show is taped.
Time: The present.

(Backstage in the dressing room of a television talk show host, during a commercial break of a taping of the show. DENISE, a hairdresser, and LAINIE, a wardrobe attendant, are poised waiting with hairbrush, hairspray, clothes brush and baby wipes in hand. A clothes rack is there, with street clothes and a suit all set up. TISH, the talk show host, enters wearing another on-air outfit. She's really a smart, pretty, nice, normal person, not a diva at all. DENISE and LAINIE are on her like the pit crew at an auto race.)

DENISE. Turn to me.

(DENISE begins fussing with TISH's hair, combing a strand or two whenever she gets the chance.)

LAINIE. Turn to me.
DENISE. I'll fix the front.
LAINIE. There's a spot.
TISH. *(Pacing.)* They know each other.
DENISE. Just a ….
LAINIE. *(Trying to reach TISH's collar.)* Is that make-up?
TISH. They know each other.
LAINIE. I thought I saw a spot …
TISH. Just using us.
LAINIE. … on the monitor.

(TISH continues moving around, picking up papers, etc., so it's hard for the women to get to her collar and hair.)

TISH. Not their first meeting.
DENISE. Really?
TISH. No. They know each other. I hate this. I really hate this. Who found these people?
DENISE. You want me to get Amanda?
TISH. No.
DENISE. Okay.
TISH. Yes. Get Amanda. *(She turns to the mirror as DENISE starts to leave.)* What's with my hair?
DENISE. I'm going to fix the front.
TISH. Didn't you look at the monitor?
DENISE. It looked fine on the monitor.
TISH. *(Turning to LAINIE.)* Did you look at the monitor?
LAINIE. Your hair looked fine.

DENISE. I'll fix it.
TISH. Go get Amanda. Where's Bobbi?
DENISE. You ran your hands through your hair when you got off camera.
TISH. Don't let me do that.
DENISE. I'll fix it.

(DENISE starts to work on TISH's hair, nearly one strand at a time. TISH stares at the mirror.)

TISH. They've met before. I could tell. There was even a slip-up, too. *(She mimics one of the guests.)* "Everybody says we're just alike." *Who* says that? They've never met. It's a given-up-for-adoption reunion. They haven't seen each other before. Who says they're alike?
(Looks in the mirror.) Is that a spot? They know each other. They're faking it.

(TISH starts to rub at her collar.)

LAINIE. I'll get that.
TISH. Was that on the monitor?
LAINIE. It didn't show. Looked like a shadow.
TISH. What is this?
LAINIE. Make-up.
DENISE. Turn to me.
TISH. *(To DENISE.)* You got make-up on me.
DENISE. No. I did not.
TISH. It's make-up.
DENISE. I'm Hair.
LAINIE. I'll get it out.
TISH. There's make-up on my collar.
DENISE. Must've been Bobbi, then.
LAINIE. It didn't show on the monitor.
TISH. We've got half a segment to go.
LAINIE. Turn to me.
DENISE. No, wait. Look at me.
TISH. Where's Amanda. Didn't you get Amanda?

(TISH leaves.)

DENISE. *(To LAINIE.)* Don't ever do that.
LAINIE. What?
DENISE. Don't ever tell her her hair looks fine.
LAINIE. She asked.
DENISE. *I* tell her her hair looks fine.

LAINIE. She asked me. What am I supposed to do? Not say anything? She'll think it looks bad. Her hair. If I don't say anything. When she asks me. Don't make such a big deal out of it.

DENISE. Don't tell me how to do my job.

LAINIE. I'm not.

DENISE. Yes, you are.

LAINIE. I'm not telling you how to do your job. But when she asks me, I tell her it looks fine. Even when it doesn't.

DENISE. You don't give me enough time with her.

LAINIE. You get a half hour with her. I get twenty seconds to get her dressed, and you're still combing and spraying.

DENISE. She likes her hair combed at the last minute.

LAINIE. Well, don't spray her when I'm trying to get her collar straight.

DENISE. She likes spray right before camera.

LAINIE. You're spraying it in my eyes. It gums up my contact lenses.

DENISE. Well, don't wear them, then. I have to spray her.

(TISH storms in, followed by AMANDA, a segment producer.)

TISH. We're not airing this.

AMANDA. Reunions are our most popular stories.

TISH. Amanda. Amanda. Amanda. We are not airing this. These people are faking it.

AMANDA. We don't know that.

TISH. Yes, we do know that. Am I the only one that knows that? I don't think so. But I know that I know. They are faking.

AMANDA. You don't know that for certain.

TISH. Oh, come on. You can tell. You can tell they are faking it. They're just acting. They've met before. You can tell. Just wanted a free trip to New York. *(Looks in the mirror.)* What's with my hair? *(Starts fussing with her bangs. DENISE races to her.)* Ride the limo to the airport. Free vacation. Get on television.

AMANDA. Is that a spot?

TISH. Where?

DENISE. Lainie, there's a spot.

LAINIE. *(Jumping in with a baby wipe.)* It's make-up.

AMANDA. *(To DENISE.)* There's make-up on her collar.

LAINIE. I'm getting it.

DENISE. I didn't do it.

AMANDA. You can't even see it.

DENISE. Must've been Bobbi.

LAINIE. The daughter hugged Tish. It's her lipstick.

TISH. When she hugged me. That was so fake. *(To DENISE and LAINIE.)* Didn't you think they were faking?

LAINIE. I didn't notice.

DENISE. I thought something was phony.

TISH. Okay, okay, okay. We're not airing this.

AMANDA. We're a couple shows behind.

TISH. We are not airing this. Final. Period. Okay. Which show is next?

AMANDA. Okay.

TISH. Good.

AMANDA. But we have to finish the segment.

TISH. No. We are not airing this.

AMANDA. Okay. But we have to finish taping.

TISH. Why? Why do we have to finish? Why do we have to finish a show we are not going to air? A show with phony people on it. With a mother who gave up her daughter at birth and wanted to find her again. And then took advantage of us. They are using us. I'm not going back out there. With that, that, that *mother!* And the daughter's wearing too much make-up. Who did her make-up? *(Looks in the mirror.)* Where's Make-up? I need a touch-up. Where's Make-up?

DENISE. I'll get her.

(DENISE races out. LAINIE takes advantage of her absence to attend to the spot.)

TISH. She should be here. Do I have to do everything? Do I have to do the research? Find the guests? Make certain they DON'T KNOW EACH OTHER AHEAD OF TIME? Do I have to do everything? Do I have to decide that THIS SEGMENT WILL NOT AIR?

AMANDA. Just finish it.

TISH. No.

AMANDA. *(No big deal.)* Just get it in the can. As a back up.

TISH. If I finish it you'll air it.

AMANDA. Just as a backup.

TISH. Use a rerun as a backup.

AMANDA. Just finish it.

TISH. No. What's with my hair? Where's Denise? *(Looks at LAINIE.)* Where's Denise?

LAINIE. She went to get Bobbi.

TISH. Why isn't Bobbi here?

AMANDA. She's doing the talent.

TISH. Talent. Right. Those fakers. What's with my hair? What's with this spot?

LAINIE. It's make-up. I'm working on it.

(DENISE and BOBBI enter. Both run over to TISH, various brushes

in hand. There is no room for LAINIE.)

TISH. What's with my hair?
DENISE. I haven't had a chance to fix it.
TISH. It's not working.
DENISE. You need a trim.
TISH. I'm growing it out.
DENISE. I'll fix it.
TISH. *(To BOBBI.)* Something's wrong with my eyes.
BOBBI. I'm fixing it.
AMANDA. I'm calling five minutes to go back to tape.
TISH. We're not airing this. This is the last straw. I am a journalist. This used to be a news show. A closer look at current events. In-depth coverage. Money issues. Health issues. Breast cancer. We used to save people's lives. What is this, this, this, garbage that they call news?
AMANDA. Breast cancer doesn't sell.
TISH. We get hundred of letters when we do cancer shows.
AMANDA. We don't get the ratings.
TISH. Can we get this spot?
LAINIE. Working on it.
TISH. Well get it!

(TISH spits on her own finger and rubs the spot, turning her back to the audience.)

LAINIE. Don't. I'm getting it ....

(TISH is facing upstage. We see on everyone's faces that the spot is much worse. There is a pause.)

AMANDA. We'll have to change jackets.
LAINIE. It's the middle of a show.
AMANDA. *(To DENISE.)* Change her jacket.
DENISE. I'm not Wardrobe.
AMANDA. Well, someone change her jacket! Give her a new jacket!
LAINIE. The tape won't match.
AMANDA. I don't care if the tape doesn't match.
TISH. *(To LAINIE.)* We're not airing the show anyway.
AMANDA. *(Tugging at TISH's jacket.)* I don't care if the tape doesn't match. We are finishing this segment and we are moving on before we lose our audience energy and before we go into overtime. *(AMANDA has pulled the jacket off TISH and hands it to LAINIE. We never see how bad the stain got.)* We will be back on the air in two minutes. I'll be in the control booth.

LAINIE. I don't have another jacket.

AMANDA. You've got a closet full of jackets. Here's a jacket.

(She grabs the one hanging in preparation for the next show.)

TISH. We're moving on to the next segment.

LAINIE. It won't match the skirt.

AMANDA. We'll shoot from the waist up. Get her in the jacket.

LAINIE. What do I use in the second show? What does she wear in the second show if I use the jacket now?

AMANDA. I don't care. You're Wardrobe. You figure it out.

LAINIE. I'm not the Designer.

AMANDA. She will finish this segment and she will shoot another one. I don't care what she wears. She can keep the other jacket on.

LAINIE. Are the shows back to back?

AMANDA. No.

LAINIE. She can wear the jacket twice if they're not airing back to back.

AMANDA. Good. *(To LAINIE, DENISE and BOBBI.)* You have one minute.

(AMANDA sorts through some papers, looking for the next script. The pit crew of LAINIE, DENISE and BOBBI all go to work at their various jobs. LAINIE holds out the jacket, BOBBIE uses a lip brush, DENISE begins to spray.)

LAINIE. You're getting it in my eyes.

DENISE. Sorry.

BOBBI. Give me a minute for her lips.

DENISE. We don't have a minute.

LAINIE. Got to get this jacket on her.

(AMANDA finds the script she was looking for and sets it down as she starts to leave.)

AMANDA. I'll be in the control room.

TISH. Wait, wait, wait, wait, wait. *(She waves everyone away. To AMANDA.)* This is my show. Mine. Mine. Mine. My show.

(DENISE, LAINIIE and BOBBI stand back in shock.)

AMANDA. *(Off-handedly, humoring her.)* Of course it's your show, Tish.

TISH. Mine. And I'm not going to let some little girl barely past her internship tell me what to do.

AMANDA. I'm your producer, Tish.

TISH. You are an associate producer. Where's Deborah?

AMANDA. Deborah's in Paris. You got the e-mail.

TISH. I have been working professionally for twenty years. Twenty years!

DENISE. *(Whispering aside to LAINIE and BOBBI.)* You'd think she was prime time.

TISH. *(To AMANDA.)* I've been a journalist since before you even started your period. When "e" stood for "ethics" not "e-mail." So some little sorority girl playing television is not going to tell me what to do on my show. My show. Do you get it? Do you want to keep your job?

AMANDA. Fine.

TISH. Fine. Okay. We're moving on.

(DENISE, LAINIE and BOBBI descend on her. LAINIE is using a lint brush. DENISE has a cordless curling iron in one hand and a brush in the other. BOBBI waves a make-up brush, trying to get to TISH.)

TISH. What's next on the show?

BOBBI. Turn to me.

LAINIE. *(Overlapping.)* Turn to me.

DENISE. *Overlapping.)* Let me fix the front.

TISH. *(Overlapping.)* What's the next show? What's the next show? After the adopted fakers?

AMANDA. *(Handing her a script.)* It's trendy. Edgy.

TISH. *(Reads from her paper.)* "Branding." What's this? I don't remember prep for this. What's branding? Brand names? Branding? People addicted to brand names? Didn't we do that show?

AMANDA. It's people who've been branded.

TISH. Branded?

(TISH turns to BOBBI, who is compelled to speak.)

BOBBI. They're in the make-up room comparing their brands. It's like tattoos. Only with a hot branding iron.

TISH. You're kidding me, right. You're kidding me.

BOBBI. No.

TISH. No.

(The room is silent.)

AMANDA. You've got five minutes. I'll tell the talent to get ready.

(DENISE, LAINIE and BOBBI go furiously to work on TISH.)

TISH. No.
AMANDA. You wanted the next show. You're getting the next show.

(AMANDA starts to leave. TISH grabs AMANDA with one hand and DENISE's curling iron with the other.)

TISH. I'll show you branding! *(TISH places the hot curling iron on AMANDA's arm and holds it there. AMANDA screams. The three other women shrink back. TISH lets go of AMANDA. There is a shocked silence. TISH hands the curling iron back to DENISE and fixes the front of her hair in the mirror.)* The next segment will be about, about people who mutilate themselves. *(She takes one last look in the mirror.)* I don't need any notes. I don't even need any guests.

(TISH exits. AMANDA stands with her mouth hanging open, holding her arm, staring after TISH. No one says a word. DENISE looks in the mirror and straightens her hair. BOBBI touches up her own make-up, while LAINIE picks lint off her own clothes.)

AMANDA. Do you have any ice?
DENISE. *(Looking in the mirror and curling her own hair with the curling iron.)* That's not our department. That's Props. Props has ice.

END OF THE PLAY

SET DESCRIPTION

Makeup table downstage so that the characters look at the audience
    when they are looking in the "mirror"
Clothes rack
A small sofa or comfortable chair
Side table

PROPERTIES

Blue index cards
File folders
Papers
Water bottle
Soda can
Plate with half a sandwich on it
Hairbrush
Hairspray
Blow dryer
Combs
Cordless curling iron

Makeup
Makeup brushes
Clothes brush
Baby wipes
Safety pins
Makeup kit
Tote bag with brushes, hairsprays
Wardrobe box or kit with thread,
    etc.
Women's suits on hangers
Jackets on hangers

COSTUMES

DENISE
    Black skirt or pants
    Black top
    Trendy shoes

LAINIE
    Shapeless dress
    Smock with safety pins on it
    Comfortable shoes

BOBBIE
    Dark oversized sweater
    Black pants or leggings
    Sneakers

TISH
    Bright anchor-woman jacket
    Blouse
    Short skirt or slacks
    Pumps
    Earrings

AMANDA
    Sweater set
    Skirt
    Smart pumps
    Pearls

A PEACE REPLACED

by

Brian Maloney

This story is dedicated to the donor families across the land
who selflessly offer another chance at life
in ultimate remembrance of their loved ones lost.

With thanks to director, Gary Wolf,
for all his support and sensitivity
in bringing this idea to script, then stage.

A PEACE REPLACED was originally produced by Emerging Artists Theatre Group (Paul Adams, Artistic Director) at the Intar Theatre in New York City in their Fall One-Act Festival in November of 2000. The play was directed by Dave Winitsky. The cast:

MAITE BARCOS...Hanna Hayes

TIM REILLY...Doug Baron

A PEACE REPLACED was subsequently produced at the American Theatre of Actors in New York City in August of 2001, directed by Gary Wolf with the following cast:

MAITE BARCOS...Teresa Yenque

TIM REILLY...Robert O'Gorman

ABOUT THE AUTHOR

BRIAN MALONEY studied theater at Montclair State University, playwriting at Playwrights Horizons with James Ryan, and script analysis with Deborah Mathiew Byers. Based on his true life experience, *A PEACE REPLACED* won first place in the Strawberry One-Act Festival in the summer of 2000 and, later that year, was accepted into Emerging Artists Theatre Group's Fall Festival. The play was performed in June of 2001 at the national convention of the Organ Procurement Organization.

CHARACTERS

MAITE BARCOS: a widow, originally from Columbia.
TIM REILLY: a middle-aged man who has received a liver transplant.

SETTING:

Place: Bricktown, New Jersey
Time: Springtime, 1999

(A woman is sitting at the kitchen table; she gets up and checks her cooking. Fixes place mats nervously and waits. The doorbell rings and she fixes herself up. She walks to the door, opens it, and a middle age man enters.

She stares at his eyes, he looks at her, then the floor, then back at her. They start to hug, then break away like strangers, recompose themselves, and introduce each other. MAITE speaks with a Spanish accent.)

MAITE. It's very odd. It's difficult.

TIM. Complex.

MAITE. Yes, complex. I am Maite Barcos.

TIM. Tim Reilly. Very nice to meet you.

MAITE. So a piece of him lives with you.

TIM. With me! Yes exactly.

MAITE. I miss him terribly.

TIM. I know. It's hard for me not to think of. That you and your children lost him, and that he lost you and I get these feelings. I am driven sometimes in directions that I wasn't before; I knew I had to meet you. And I suppose that I feel he is with me.

MAITE. But you didn't even know him Mr. Reilly. I have constant reminders of him.

TIM. Me to. Not reminders exactly.

MAITE. The worst thing was I wasn't with him, we never said goodbye.

TIM. Tell me about him.

MAITE. Why?

TIM. It's just important to me. Did you always live here?

MAITE. He moved us out of the city so the children could have a better life.

TIM. It's a beautiful home.

MAITE. It means nothing.

TIM. No! It's a better place. Better.

MAITE. No, this is what *we* wanted. This was *our* dream.

TIM. You could go back, to the city. Talk to me about him.

MAITE. He gave you another chance.

TIM. Yes he did. Tell me about Jorge. Talk to me about your relationship.

MAITE. This …. I don't feel this is appropriate for you to ask me these questions. I don't even know you Mr. Reilly, not really.

TIM. Tim.

MAITE. I prefer Mr. Reilly.

TIM. He gave me his liver but sometimes it feels like more than that. What about you Maite? What is your story?

MAITE. It's not important.

TIM. It is to me.

MAITE. It's none of your business.

TIM. I feel it would help me to understand. Please.

MAITE. Understand what?

TIM. This new life.

MAITE. Miguel is my first son. Miguel's father was a bum. He is older. My parents made me marry him even though I didn't want to. That was in Bogata. When I brought my son to this country I was completely alone for fourteen years. I was content to be alone, the last thing I wanted was another man.

TIM. How did you two meet?

MAITE. I worked in a hospital. He was there doing construction for two months. He came to my desk to ask me out. I told him I would never go out with a Puerto Rican. He left me alone. At the end of his time working there he came and asked for my telephone number; I gave it to him, he held both my shoulders firmly, kissed me, looked in my eyes and said; "Thank you Maite." Nine months after that I married him.

TIM. How about that.

MAITE. *(Tearing.)* Words can not describe what we had, how much we were equally 'in love' the last fifteen years.

TIM. What was it like?

MAITE. Nothing was too good for me. I know I am old fashioned but this man would come around the car and open my door from the day I met him until the day he left me. He gave me the best of everything. *(Pause.)* I came to this country with nothing, I was stingy and greedy, I was miserly — with every nickel. From the day we were married he told me it was better to give than to receive. He was boyish that way.

TIM. This conversation, this meeting, is sacred to me. I feel so curious. *(TIM goes to a table and removes a picture.)* Is this Jorge?

MAITE. Put that back!

TIM. I'm sorry, I wanted to see him.

MAITE. Then ask me. My husband had manners. *(MAITE snaps the picture from his hand, stares at it for a moment, and puts it back on the table.)* White people think they can take anything.

TIM. Forgive me. Are there other photographs?

(MAITE pulls out a box and begins to take items out to show TIM.)

MAITE. These were his glasses. *(MAITE places the glasses on the table. TIM picks up the glasses and tries them on. MAITE snaps them off his face and puts them back in the box. She takes a picture album out of the box and opens to the first page.)* This is him with his two best friends. They shared everything with each other.

TIM. Is this picture from Puerto Rico?

MAITE. They were soldiers. In Vietnam. One is Spanish, one is not.

TIM. I've had the dreams, very powerful dreams. But I wasn't there.

(MAITE turns the page.)

MAITE. Do you have children?

TIM. One boy, one girl.

MAITE. Jorge and I have little George and Marie. My son Miguel was born in Bogata, I told you about him.

TIM. Yes.

MAITE. This is Miguel and his wife. She is a black, black woman.

TIM. I can see that. She is the one here in the white, white dress.

MAITE. This picture is from the 'famous wedding.'

TIM. Famous?

MAITE. Only to me, and Jorge and maybe Miguel. My mother looked down on certain kinds of people, her head almost exploded when I told her I was marrying a Puerto Rican. She was furious back then. She forbade me to marry Jorge. She made me marry a drunk, back in Bogata, but to marry Jorge, who treated me like a princess.... Turn the page. *(TIM turns the page on the photo album.)* Now you see my mother with her *new* favorite son, Jorge, together at the famous wedding. He could change anyone just from his disposition, from the love in his heart. But, I turned into my mother from ten years before. I had become a worse racist then her. I told my son, with whom all we had was each other all those years, 'demanded' from my loving beautiful Miguel, that he not marry his woman. I forbade him. I told him that I would not come to the wedding and never see him again if he did this to me! I was horrible. One week before the wedding Jorge comes home from work that day and calls to me; Naegra!, this was his pet name for me. Naegra! Sit down, he says. I sit with him and he tells me: If you are not at this wedding at Miguel's side and this marriage does not work out, Miguel will have no where to come home to. And if they stay together it will mean that our Miguel has found the love. And what mother would not want this for her son. He changed me again, better to give, sí?

(TIM holds his hands together as though he is praying and shakes them forward. He does this whenever he understands or agrees.)

TIM. Sí.

MAITE. The children went to their uncle for dinner.

TIM. May I take you out for some supper?

MAITE. I won't eat in a restaurant.

TIM. Ever?

MAITE. Never. You can eat with me if you like. I have cooked Jorge's favorite Puerto Rican dish, with the rice and beans.

TIM. Sounds great. Do you cook often?

(MAITE gets up to warm up the meal.)

MAITE. Every day. And I know every day what I am eating.

TIM. Did Jorge eat in restaurants?

MAITE He was too trusting. But he always came home for dinner.

TIM Was he a fisherman?

MAITE. No.

TIM. An artist, a painter?

MAITE. He loved two things. His family and people.

TIM. I knew the first.

MAITE. Yes, you said that in your letter. What else do you know?

TIM. I had to see you. I had to come here to see how you and the children are doing. I need this.

MAITE. You assume too much Mr. Reilly.

TIM. Tim.

MAITE. Do you like spicy?

TIM. Make it just the way he liked it.

(MAITE turns and faces TIM.)

MAITE. What do you want Mr. Reilly?

(Pause.)

TIM. *(Unsure.)* I want to help you. I feel I came for him. And, I want you to know this wasn't a waste. I was not a waste.

MAITE. Mr. Reilly. Tim, you have shown me this. Don't push yourself on me. My husband is dead. What do you really want with knowing all about him, and me, you owe us nothing. Is it guilt you're feeling?

TIM. No!

MAITE. Then why do you want your food to taste like his. Why do you feel you have to watch his children? What is next Mr. Reilly? Are you going to want me?

TIM. No!

MAITE. Then why? You sound strange, you could be perceived wrong.

TIM. No. Its not what you think.

MAITE. It doesn't matter what I think.

TIM. It's all that matters. I have doubted myself, my transplant.

MAITE. What do you mean?

TIM. Sometimes I am afraid I may have been too eager. I pushed for it and I feel like I may have even faked my symptoms a little. I'm sorry.

(MAITE sits.)

MAITE. Let me tell you something. *(Long pause.)* I have worked in one hospital or another for the last twenty-one years. The doctors don't give you an organ transplant because you are faking. There are tests that they take and blood work.

TIM. I know.

MAITE. Then what are you saying?

TIM. I have never told anyone this but I have felt worse since the transplant. I cant get any peace, I don't think I will ever be the same again. Maybe if I had waited. I wonder about the timing. Why did I line up with Jorge's death? Why not someone else?

MAITE. So ... you are the one who doesn't know if it was worth it.

(TIM drops his head.)

TIM. I suppose.

MAITE. They told me you would have died without it, is that true?

TIM. Yes.

(MAITE walks over and takes him by the collar and drags him out of the chair.)

MAITE. You listen to me now! If my Jorge had to leave his family behind. You will not leave yours. You pull yourself up gringo. You stop feeling sorry for yourself. You said in your letter you knew that Jorge was a fighter. Well — you're right! And now its time for you to fight. You want to know if you had waited would fate had given you a different liver, a better liver?

TIM. Yes.

MAITE. Well my husband didn't die for you. He died because he died, and if you think there is more to it than that you are crazy! I don't believe in such nonsense. Jorge wondered about these things and look where it got him, nowhere. He is gone. Then he, we, gave you a chance. And you better take it Mr. Reilly! *(She dishes him out some rice and beans drops the bowl and silverware in front of him.)*

That's how he likes it, if that is what you're asking. *(They sit and eat in silence for a minute.)* So what will you do now?

TIM. I don't know. Go home I guess. Be there for my kids. Be with my family. Find a woman to love and treat her like nothing is too good for her. I want the love.

MAITE. Did you know that I never had a chance to say goodbye? I left him for five minutes, when I came back, he was already dead.

TIM. I don't want you to be afraid.

MAITE. He died instantly. He had a brain aneurysm.

TIM. I know now why I really came, don't you?

MAITE. Are you asking me to believe ... that my husband sent you?

(TIM stops eating and looks at her.)

TIM. I am carrying with me here, today, something .... Believe what you want to believe there is more to this, more to him than just a liver. The me, the way I was my whole life, is gone now.

MAITE. Did you always do this?

(MAITE shakes her hands as he has been doing.)

TIM. Please acknowledge this Maite. Please let him ... let this happen.

MAITE. How is the food? Is it hot enough?

(TIM sits straight up, tilts his head back and closes his eyes for a moment.)

TIM. Open your heart.

MAITE. I don't believe in any kind of nonsense. My husband is gone.

TIM. Ask God to help you Maite.

MAITE. God left me with nothing. There is no God for me.

TIM. Pray. And I'll pray for you.

MAITE. Don't pray for me!

TIM. Please!

(TIM sobs about his failure.)

MAITE. You don't like the food?

TIM. The food is great but I can feel it's time for me to go. I'm sorry.

MAITE. Are you all right?

TIM. Yes. I need to go home and rest a while.

(They sit in silence for a long moment. TIM gets up to leave.)

MAITE. Wait. *(TIM looks at her. MAITE looks at him, she walks to the table and takes Jorge's picture in her hand, looks at it, then holds it close to her heart. She then walks up close to TIM and puts the picture in his pocket. She places her hands on his shoulders.)* Better to give. Sí?

TIM. Thank you Maite.

(MAITE places a hand over TIM's eyes, closes her eyes, leans in and gives TIM a long, still, but passionate kiss on the lips.)

MAITE. Goodbye my love.

(TIM tries to speak and MAITE places her index finger over his lips , walks him to the door and opens it. TIM exits. MAITE closes the door then leans face first into it.
Memorable music begins.
MAITE returns to the table and sits looking slowly through the pages of her picture album.
Music volume rises as a single light focuses on MAITE, then slowly fades to black.)

END OF THE PLAY

SET DESCRIPTION

Kitchen table with 2 chairs
Small table for picture of Jorge (and box)
Tablecloth
Water pitcher and 2 glasses
2 placemats
2 forks, 2 knives and 2 napkins

Makeshift stove top
1 pot, I pan, 2 dishes and 1 serving spoon

Doorbell

PROPERTIES

Pocket-size frame and picture of Jorge
Nice box for Jorge memorabilia
Jorge's eyeglasses
Photo album with Maite's memories

COSTUMES

MAITE is dressed for company.

TIM wears loose-fitting pants, shoes for comfort and a blazer that
    once fit but is now too large.

THREE TABLES

by

Dan Remmes

*This play is dedicated to anyone
who has ever been in a relationship.*

THREE TABLES was present by Mind The Gap Theatre in August, 2001 under the direction of Paula D'Alessandris. The set was designed by Kristin Costa. The cast:

MANDY	Susan Cameron
PAUL	Eric Giancoli
BARBARA	Susan Estes
MICHAEL	Dan Remmes
DORIS	Kathy Searle
TODD	Stephen Donovan
WAITER	Joshua Knapp

ABOUT THE AUTHOR

DAN REMMES plays have been produced in fourteen cities and seven states, won or placed in ten national/international writing competitions and featured Emmy and Obie-winning actors.

CHARACTERS

While it is ideal for all couples to be in their thirties, there are no age restrictions provided it doesn't strain the credibility of the dialogue or circumstance. The Waiter may be any age or gender.

SETTING

Place: An upscale restaurant.
Time: Evening.

(Three 'tables for two' are on stage: one left, one center, one right. While focus is typically on one table at a time, the remaining two sustain activity, silently pantomiming conversation when without written dialogue.

At the stage right table sit PAUL and MANDY. MICHAEL sits alone in the center table, perusing a menu, while DORIS and TODD converse silently stage left. It might be appropriate for all characters to be in their thirties, but this is flexible provided it doesn't strain credibility of the situation. Seating arrangements at each table will be determined by the dialogue and become self-evident.

AT RISE: Our focus begins stage right, with MANDY and PAUL sipping wine.)

MANDY. You look very handsome this evening.

PAUL. You, my dear, are a painting.

MANDY. I love this place.

PAUL. Yeah.

MANDY. I don't care how full I get, we're having that cake for dessert. What was it called?

PAUL. Assassination by Chocolate.

MANDY. *(Seductively.)* Only one thing in life is better.

PAUL. *(Equally flirtatious.)* I think I know what that is.

MANDY. The Apple Strudel at Gregory's.

PAUL. Right. Well. Not what I was going to say, but I'll force that argument later.

MANDY. *(Warmly.)* I look forward to the debate.

(PAUL produces a small, perfectly wrapped gift and presents it to MANDY.)

PAUL. I got you something.

MANDY. Paul! You said we weren't going to exchange gifts!

PAUL. I know. I couldn't help it. Happy anniversary.

MANDY. What is it?

PAUL. Open it.

MANDY. *(As she opens the gift.)* I don't believe you did this.

PAUL. It's no big deal. For our fifth anniversary, you deserve something more than just dinner.

(Inside is a petite silver necklace.)

MANDY. Oh, Paul, it's beautiful.

PAUL. Put it on.

MANDY. It's just — thank you so much. It's perfect.

(She models the necklace.)

PAUL. I know you don't wear a lot of jewelry, but it looks so good on you.

MANDY. Thank you, sweetheart. Very much. What a nice surprise. *(Beat.)* Okay, I got you something too.

PAUL. You faker! What is it?

(From her purse she produces a white envelope.)

MANDY. It's a card. I took the no-gift thing literally.

PAUL. Oh.

MANDY. Open it.

PAUL. Okay. *(He does, reading.)* "On our Wooden Anniversary." Wooden? Is that what the fifth anniversary is?

MANDY. Uh, huh.

PAUL. I didn't know that. *(He opens the card and reads aloud.)*

"Wooden anniversaries
Make gift-giving hard
So rather than pencils
I bought you this card."

That's so — sweet.

MANDY. Pencils are made of wood. Get it?

PAUL. I got that.

MANDY. I wrote something else — there. Under that.

PAUL. "To my darling husband. Thank you for the best five years of my life. I love you more than anything, and I always will. Mandy." Oh, sweetheart. That's very thoughtful. I love you too. Happy Anniversary.

(PAUL leans over the table and kisses his wife. As he does so, BARBARA, an intent business woman, enters hastily with a portfolio of papers. She sits at the center table opposite MICHAEL, where focus now shifts.)

BARBARA. What are we doing here?

MICHAEL. I like to think of it as the last supper.

BARBARA. Just sign the papers and be done with it.

MICHAEL. I don't want to sign the papers.

BARBARA. Oh, so *that's* why we're meeting in public. So you'll have witnesses when I strangle you.

MICHAEL. Can we speak civilly for a moment?

BARBARA. I'm not eating dinner with you.

(A WAITER enters and approaches.)

WAITER. Can I get you folks a drink?

BARBARA. *(To WAITER.)* Nothing for me. I'm leaving in a few seconds.

MICHAEL. Could we have two glasses of Chardonnay and — *(To BARBARA.)* — do you want to split a salad?

BARBARA. Just a glass of water. And you can take the menu. I'm not eating.

MICHAEL. Make that a bottle of Chardonnay and a large Caesar's salad, no anchovies.

BARBARA. You know I like the an—

MICHAEL. That's right. Anchovies. Lots of anchovies.

BARBARA. NO! I mean — get what you want. I'm not staying.

(The WAITER departs.)

MICHAEL. I'm not signing anything until you have a glass of wine and a plate of romaine. And here — *(He takes a roll from the basket of bread and breaks it in half, ceremoniously.)* This is my body, which will be given up ... for you.

BARBARA. Every so often I ask myself why I'm divorcing you. All it takes is thirty seconds in your presence.

MICHAEL. I don't want to get divorced.

BARBARA. You better not be wasting my time.

MICHAEL. Let's just talk about it some more.

BARBARA. After three years, now you want to talk. How come you never wanted to talk when *I* wanted to talk. God knows you never wanted to talk when the Giants were on television.

MICHAEL. I sold the satellite dish.

BARBARA. Just sign the damned — You what?

MICHAEL. Yeah. No more sports. Okay, well, some sports. I still have regular cable.

BARBARA. You got rid of the satellite dish?

MICHAEL. I know. I was a little preoccupied with television.

BARBARA. I'm surprised this agreement doesn't include custody of the remote.

MICHAEL. That's very clever.

BARBARA. So what prompted that?

MICHAEL. *(Tenderly.)* Barbara, I want you more than I want televised sports.

BARBARA. I'm swooning.

MICHAEL. Let's just have a nice dinner and when we're done eating, if you still want me to sign the papers, I'll sign the papers.

BARBARA. This is not a negotiating table, Michael. That part is over. *(Demonstrating.)* There are seven documents in triplicate. I need you to initial the highlighted boxes, then sign the bottom of each.

MICHAEL. Why are you being difficult?

BARBARA. *(Beside herself.)* Are you crazy? I spent all three years of our marriage being understanding, conciliatory and appreciative of what little attention I got.

MICHAEL. I got rid of the satellite dish.

BARBARA. I hope you have another card to play because I've seen that one already.

MICHAEL. I want to change. I want to make this work.

BARBARA. You're unbelievable.

MICHAEL. What else can I change? Tell me. I'm open to it.

BARBARA. Okay. Improve your hearing. It's over.

MICHAEL. I love you.

BARBARA. Too little too late.

MICHAEL. My loving you is too little?

BARBARA. It's half of what a marriage requires.

MICHAEL. *(Facetiously.)* Waiter, another knife please? Hers is stuck in my heart.

BARBARA. Sign the papers.

MICHAEL. I haven't watched a single basketball game since you left.

BARBARA. Because it's baseball season. And it's not just the sports, Michael. It's a profound inability to communicate.

MICHAEL. I'm communicating now. I sold the satellite dish, I've given up sports, and I'm having a conversation. This, right now, is communication. What else can I do? Talk to me.

BARBARA. Okay, *why* do you love me?

MICHAEL. Because you're beautiful, you're smart, and you're understanding.

BARBARA. Understanding. Right. Not enough to spend eight thousand dollars on divorce proceedings to scrap them over a six dollar salad.

(The WAITER arrives with the salad.)

MICHAEL. *(To WAITER, desperately.)* And wine. I ordered wine too. Quickly, please.

BARBARA. Are you going to sign these papers or not? I can have you subpoenaed if you prefer.

MICHAEL. I love you.

BARBARA. Show me how much; sign this divorce.

(The argument continues in silent, subtle mime as focus shifts to the stage left table, DORIS and TODD.)

DORIS. So am I what you were expecting?

TODD. I already saw your photograph.

DORIS. I know. But I obviously scanned the best photo I had of myself.

TODD. It was a nice photo. A very beautiful photo.

(Beat.)

DORIS. So you're disappointed.

TODD. Oh, no. Not at all. I'm sorry. You're very attractive in person as well.

DORIS. That photo was a couple of years old.

TODD. So was mine.

DORIS. My hair was different.

TODD. Very different.

DORIS. I was going through a phase.

TODD. That's okay.

DORIS. You look a lot like your photo too. Except that you're alone now.

TODD. Yeah, I was debating whether to crop out my old girlfriend, but I'm not very good with that editing software.

DORIS. That's okay.

TODD. I tried to, you know, airbrush her — work her into the surrounding foliage. But it looked like a deformed shrub in high heels, so I decided —

DORIS. I'm not very good with the computer either.

TODD. Anyway, don't read into it.

DORIS. She's a very attractive woman, your ex-girlfriend.

TODD. Thank you.

(Beat.)

DORIS. So am I what you were expecting?

TODD. Didn't we just have this conversation?

DORIS. I mean my demeanor. The overall presentation.

TODD. Oh. Well, to tell you the truth, I don't think I've gathered enough data yet. We're only in the cocktail phase. Ask me again during dessert.

DORIS. Will do.

TODD. So you're a lawyer.

DORIS. An attorney.

TODD. My mistake.

DORIS. I don't like lawyer jokes so I prefer the term "attorney." Nobody tells attorney jokes.

TODD. What's sad about a car full of lawyers going over a cliff?

DORIS. There's an empty seat. I've heard them all.

TODD. What do you call ten *attorneys* at the bottom of the

ocean?

DORIS. A good start.

TODD. Are we having a good start, do you think?

DORIS. I'll know better once you field a couple of shrink jokes.

TODD. I prefer "therapist."

DORIS. What do you call a shrink okay never mind. *(Beat.)* So, have you ever done this before?

TODD. Date?

DORIS. Blind date. Met someone on the internet.

TODD. Which one, counselor? A blind date, or met someone on the internet?

DORIS. Let me rephrase the question. Have you ever gone on a blind date with someone you met on the internet?

TODD. No.

DORIS. Me neither.

TODD. Actually, I lied. You're my seventh.

DORIS. Oh, my.

TODD. Yeah.

DORIS. Your seventh? I'm —

TODD. Flabbergasted? You can leave now if you want.

DORIS. No! It's not that, it's just — Well, here I've been thinking it was still somewhat taboo. The whole internet dating thing.

TODD. I seem to have overcome the taboo.

DORIS. Apparently.

TODD. You think less of me now?

DORIS. No —

TODD. You think I'm a strumpet?

DORIS. A strumpet? Well, no, of course n— I'm not even sure I know what that word means.

TODD. So why did you agree to go out with me if you didn't like the photo?

DORIS. I figured the woman you were with was your sister.

TODD. We're a different race.

DORIS. She was adopted. Defense attorneys are good at rationalization.

TODD. Of course.

DORIS. Logically, I figured you wouldn't have placed an ad on LoveLorn.com if you were still with your girlfriend.

TODD. That makes sense.

DORIS. And what led you to send a picture of your ex-girlfriend to someone you're attempting to woo.

TODD. I told you, I couldn't use the cropping software.

DORIS. You have no photos of yourself without your ex-girlfriend?

TODD. Not many. We were together for ten years.

DORIS. I knew there'd be something.

TODD. What?

DORIS. You're still hung up on her.

TODD. No. Really, I'm not.

DORIS. You're still hung up on her, that's why you've dated seven other women from the internet and none of them worked out.

TODD. That's not the reason at all. For example, one of them just didn't look like her photo.

DORIS. That's why I sent a picture that was two years old. Men are so superficial.

TODD. No. She e-mailed a photo of a completely different person. She told me she didn't think I'd mind once I met and got to know her.

DORIS. Was she right?

TODD. She was a man.

DORIS. Oh.

TODD. Then there was Carletta, who had a fourteen-word vocabulary, only six of which are appropriate for broadcast television.

DORIS. But –

TODD. I know. E-mail, right? I was unwittingly corresponding with her married friend who has a Ph.D. in literature and offered to help her meet someone.

DORIS. Oh, that's sweet. Like Cyrano DeBergerac.

TODD. Right. Only it wasn't her nose that was big.

DORIS. I see. *(Long beat. She can't take it.)* What was it?

TODD. First words out of her mouth: "Like my big tits?" Truth be told, I did. They arrived ten minutes before she did. But call me old fashioned, I'd have preferred a simple "Hi, nice to meet you."

DORIS. Oh, Good. Because I almost said the other thing.

TODD. So you're an attractive, intelligent woman. What was the final straw that led you to answer a personal ad?

DORIS. My friend recommended it. She met her husband on the internet and I've been so busy with my new practice there hasn't been much time for a social life. It's kind of the fast food of dating, isn't it? Here are my statistics, there are yours, the computer crunches the numbers and out pops something to do on a Saturday night.

TODD. And before this?

DORIS. There was a relationship in law school. We were engaged, as a matter of fact. A week before the ceremony I called it off.

TODD. That's encouraging.

DORIS. I almost called this off too. It took every ounce of will power I had to meet you here tonight.

TODD. So, let's see, we've got a noncommittal woman with no time for a social life partnered with a man who's done nothing but date losers and isn't quite over his ex.

DORIS. Aren't computers amazing.

(Focus returns to MANDY and PAUL, stage right.)

MANDY. What are you looking at?

PAUL. Oh, nothing. Just — *(Referring to BARBARA and MICHAEL, center.)* I was overhearing part of the conversation at the table behind you.

MANDY. I know. I heard them too. What are they talking about?

PAUL. All I can make out is the tone. They seemed pretty angry with each other. Then a salad arrived.

MANDY. How many people are there?

PAUL. It's a couple. Turn around. Look.

MANDY. I'm not going to turn around. They'll know I'm looking at them.

PAUL. No they won't. They're too wrapped up in themselves.

MANDY. Still, I can't —

PAUL. Pretend to drop your spoon or something.

MANDY. Is this the woman who walked in when we were kissing?

PAUL. I guess so.

MANDY. The very attractive woman?

PAUL. I don't know.

MANDY. That explains it.

PAUL. Explains what?

MANDY. The reason your eyes remained open when we kissed.

PAUL. No, they didn't.

MANDY. Then why were they open?

PAUL. *(Playfully.)* How do you know my eyes were open unless yours were open too?

MANDY. My eyes were open because I saw the attractive woman walk in right before we kissed, and I wanted to see if you would notice her.

PAUL. So I'm under surveillance.

MANDY. Sorry. I know.

PAUL. No, you're right. I shouldn't have looked.

MANDY. Come on. She's attractive. I looked too. I'm just being paranoid.

PAUL. Let's agree to disagree.

MANDY. No, let's agree to agree.

PAUL. You're on.

MANDY. *(Raising her glass.)* Here's to another five.

PAUL. Cheers. *(They toast. Beat.)* Are you sure number five is the wooden anniversary? Pretty sure it's cotton.

(Focus to BARBARA and MICHAEL, who are now sharing a bottle of wine.)

MICHAEL. How was the salad?

BARBARA. How do you do it? How can I be so angry with you one minute only to forget it a moment later?

MICHAEL. I buy you food.

BARBARA. Shut up.

MICHAEL. What do you say? A main course?

BARBARA. I can't.

MICHAEL. Come on. What, do you have other plans tonight or something?

BARBARA. Actually, yes.

MICHAEL. Washing your hair?

BARBARA. I have a date.

MICHAEL. *(Beat.)* What?

BARBARA. It's a first date. Someone from work.

MICHAEL. A date? My wife has a date?

BARBARA. I'm not your wife anymore.

MICHAEL. You are until I sign those papers! Barbara! How could you have a date?

BARBARA. Michael, we've been separated almost eight months.

MICHAEL. Call him up and tell him you've decided to have dinner with your husband.

BARBARA. I'm not going to do that.

MICHAEL. When are you meeting him?

BARBARA. He's picking me up in an hour.

MICHAEL. Where?

BARBARA. My apartment.

MICHAEL. That's not safe! You meet him in a brightly lit public place or you don't meet him at all.

BARBARA. It's a guy I know from work, Michael, not someone I just met on the internet!

(To DORIS and TODD.)

DORIS. – and you also had the best screen name of anyone I chatted with on line.

TODD. I like yours too. Hathaway at Hathaway and Hathaway dot com.

DORIS. Redundant, I'll admit, but easy to remember. Actually, I'm the only Hathaway. But my father was an attorney, so I figure that counts.

TODD. See, I thought the other Hathaway might be your husband and you thought my actual girlfriend might be my sister. We've got a nice little half-full/half-empty dynamic going on here.

DORIS. Are you charging me by the hour?

TODD. I won't if you won't.

DORIS. I am now prepared to declare we are having a good start.

TODD. And I'm glad I hung in there until number eight.

(They toast.)

DORIS. I still can't get over that. Were they all terrible experiences, or just those two?

TODD. No. All of them.

DORIS. So I may have dodged a bullet here.

TODD. Or you just have lower standards.

DORIS. What does that mean?

TODD. Not you personally, women in general. It's inevitable. Look at any situation comedy on television. In nine out of ten, the male lead is some sort of backwater dullard. Not difficult to live up to that standard.

DORIS. And every female lead is under 25 and perfect-looking.

TODD. Which means the aesthetic criterion for men is lower as well. And consider how you freely refer to us as snakes, jerks, apes –

DORIS. Pigs.

TODD. Has some male organization formed in attempt to amend this kind of chauvinism?

DORIS. Because men couldn't care less when they're insulted. Some actually take pride in it.

TODD. All the more reason it's easier for me to make a good impression on you.

DORIS. I'll say this much for you: We've been here half an hour and you haven't once made mention of technology or sports. Most men can't go ten minutes without discussing their favorite team or some useless gadget they've purchased for no apparent reason.

(Focus to BARBARA and MICHAEL, briefly.)

MICHAEL. Don't you understand? I gave up a dual LAB twenty-inch satellite dish with rust-resistance and auto-hone. As it is, I already missed the first three games of the regular season. For *you.*

(And we return to TODD and DORIS.)

DORIS. So what you're saying is, you're not really as great a catch as I think you are.

TODD. And you're an even *better* catch than I think *you* are.

DORIS. I'm beginning to appreciate this line of thinking.

(To MANDY and PAUL.)

MANDY. I'm telling you, it's iron.

PAUL. Iron?

MANDY. Yes.

PAUL. The sixth wedding anniversary is cotton. I may not have remembered wood, but I remember Tony's sixth anniversary and he told me it was cotton.

MANDY. Paul, I'm going to tell you this one more time, and then we're going to drop it. The sixth anniversary is the iron anniversary. I had to research it to find out about wood. If you don't believe it, look it up.

PAUL. Cotton.

MANDY. Why do you always have to have the last word? We're not going to make it to the sixth anniversary if you don't learn to let things drop. When we get home, we can look it up. End of conversation.

PAUL. Fine. *(A beat. Then, softly.)* But it's cotton.

(DORIS has been taken in by the antics two tables over. TODD notices her distraction.)

TODD. What are you looking at?

DORIS. Oh, I'm sorry. I have this bad habit of eavesdropping in restaurants.

TODD. Yeah, women love to do that.

DORIS. You know, I have no problem with you stereotyping your own gender, buddy, but don't go — what is *up* over there?

TODD. What's happening?

DORIS. You're saying you've never been to a restaurant when you're curious to know what's going on at another table? What people's relationships are to each other?

TODD. Of course I have. Human nature is my job. Stop changing the subject, what's happening?

DORIS. Take a look.

TODD. Well, I can't just turn around and stare.

DORIS. Pretend to drop your spoon or something.

TODD. I am a professional psychotherapist. I'm not going to pretend to drop my spoon in a public restaurant so I can eavesdrop on total strangers eating dinner at another table. A napkin is much more credible.

(He drops his napkin, and in picking it up gives MANDY and PAUL a long stare.)

DORIS. I've been watching their body language. They came in hand-in-hand, exchanged gifts, and now they have a subtle air of contention.

TODD. Probably their anniversary.

DORIS. Could you explain that conclusion for us mere mortals.

TODD. They were hand-in-hand and exchanged gifts so, unless they're incestuous twins celebrating their birthday, it's probably their anniversary. This is an anniversary kind of restaurant. And anniversaries are rife with emotion, good and bad.

DORIS. So while most men can't keep themselves from discussing gadgets and sports, you're a perpetual analyst.

TODD. Your honor, she's leading the witness.

(Back to MANDY and PAUL.)

PAUL. What?

MANDY. You're still checking out that woman.

PAUL. Oh, for Chrissakes, Mandy. She's attractive. She caught my eye. I'm sorry.

MANDY. You know, Paul, that's natural. I can understand that.

PAUL. Thank you.

MANDY. And maybe if I hadn't walked in on you and Rosemary liplocked at Anthony's retirement party last year I wouldn't be so sensitive to it.

PAUL. How many times do I have to say this: We didn't have sex.

MANDY. Praise Paul! He didn't have sex with his secretary. I'm surprised you didn't have that engraved on my new necklace.

PAUL. Well, at least I got you something. What did I get? On my fifth wedding anniversary. A card with a poem about a pencil. That hurts, Mandy.

MANDY. We said no gifts.

PAUL. When people say no gifts they don't really mean no gifts. Everybody knows that. Regardless of what we said, if I didn't get you a gift for our anniversary you'd be pissed!

MANDY. So was that your guiding principal? Not love. Not devotion. Avoidance of pissed.

PAUL. Well what's your excuse? Next year, on my cotton anniversary, should I look forward to new underwear or a poem about it?

MANDY. Next year, on your *iron* anniversary, you should look forward to the anvil I chain to your ankle before tossing you into the Hudson River.

PAUL. I believe the expression is "ball and chain."

(To BARBARA and MICHAEL, center. The WAITER is taking their order.)

MICHAEL. The tuna please. Rare.

BARBARA. *(To the WAITER.)* Nothing for me.

MICHAEL. She'll have the petit filet, medium.

BARBARA. *(To the WAITER, correcting.)* Medium-well.

WAITER. Very good.

(The WAITER exits.)

BARBARA. I can't believe this. I'm an hour away from a date with the head of accounting. What am I doing here with you?

MICHAEL. Oh, an accountant. That's exciting.

BARBARA. Yeah, I know. What could I say? I haven't been on a date since we separated. You have to get back on the horse sometime.

MICHAEL. I think an accountant is more of a pony.

BARBARA. He's a nice guy.

MICHAEL. I can't argue. I never met the man.

BARBARA. *(To herself.)* What am I doing? What, I'm going to have two dinners now?

MICHAEL. But the filet sounded so good. I could tell you were looking at it.

BARBARA. The mushroom sauce.

MICHAEL. Can't you just call him and tell him you're not feeling well?

BARBARA. Right. With the din of a crowded restaurant in the background. Might as well call him from Atlantic City shouting over slot machines. "Sorry Edgar, CHING CHING, I've got a real bad headache, DING DING DING DING DING."

MICHAEL. His name is Edgar?

BARBARA. *(Smiling.)* I knew you'd make an issue of that.

MICHAEL. So then you knew you'd be telling me about him at some point tonight?

BARBARA. No! Maybe. Oh, I don't know.

(She sips some wine, uncomfortably.)

MICHAEL. You realize you could never really marry someone named Edgar.

BARBARA. I'm not marrying him, we're having dinner together. *(Beat.)* As soon as I finish *this* dinner.

MICHAEL. Just call him.

BARBARA. I can't cancel a date from a restaurant.

MICHAEL. Tell him the background noise is a hospital. You're in the emergency room.

BARBARA. And the clinking silverware?

MICHAEL. Scalpels. You're holding your own entrails and will make it up to him after the transfusion.

BARBARA. *(Smirking.)* I hate you. I hate you for making me laugh.

MICHAEL. There are worse things to hate me for.

BARBARA. Oh, I've got plenty of those too.

MICHAEL. I know you do. *(A beat.)* You know what I think is really great?

BARBARA. What's that?

MICHAEL. You haven't asked me to sign those papers in over ten minutes.

(Focus moves to TODD and DORIS.)

DORIS. But then, you wonder, what's the point?

TODD. What do you mean?

DORIS. Consider that the success rate for arranged marriages – people who are randomly thrown together – is better than for couples who choose to be with each other.

TODD. So you're saying I'd have just as much chance of staying married to that woman with the tattoo reading "I brake for bitches" as I would you?

DORIS. Maybe. I mean, what do you really know about me?

TODD. Obviously you don't subscribe to this philosophy or you wouldn't have spent time comparing profiles of prospective suitors on the world wide web. Why not close your eyes and click the mouse.

DORIS. What makes you think I didn't?

TODD. So you're saying you just got lucky?

DORIS. *(Playfully.)* I don't remember saying that.

TODD. What's not taken into consideration in the statistics you quote, however, is the inherent cultural difference with arranged marriages.

DORIS. Because divorce is frowned upon much more so than in cultures where we choose our own mate.

TODD. Exactly. So the fact that fifty percent of them break up at all means a much larger percentage probably wants to and don't.

(To BARBARA and MICHAEL, whose debate has quieted somewhat.)

PAUL. No, it's my fault. I got carried away. Listen, I know things have been a little tense lately. I think it's natural at this stage of a marriage. Once the baby comes, things will settle back into a comfortable groove. A new and exciting groove.

MANDY. I don't think so.

PAUL. Sure they will.

MANDY. Let's not –

PAUL. Look, we've had our problems. But I think a lot of it is getting blown out of proportion because we want to get pregnant so badly. The frustration over that is finding its way into the most trivial of arguments and fueling them.

MANDY. Paul –

PAUL. I know what I'm talking about. I saw it happen with my brother. Now look at them. Have you ever seen a happier couple, or two more adorable children?

MANDY. But you don't know what's going on below the surface in that house.

PAUL. I tell you what. Why don't we start taking steps to remedy this. We'll go one more cycle. If you're not pregnant by this same time next month, we'll go to a specialist. I'll even volunteer to be the first one tested.

MANDY. Oh, that's chivalrous. Jerk off in a cup. Really throwing yourself in front of a train for me, there, Paul. Do you know what the *woman* has to go through for that kind of testing?

PAUL. Why are you acting like this?

MANDY. I'm just as much to blame for this relationship as anything else, I'll admit.

PAUL. What do you mean, blame?

MANDY. Who are we kidding, Paul? With this lovey-dovey anniversary crap. We're so hung up on appearances, we've tricked *ourselves* into believing we're happy.

PAUL. There've been times —

MANDY. There've been times. Sure. You don't see something wrong with the fact that it's easier to single out the handful of good times than it is to select between all the bad? *(There is no response. A beat.)* You're going to hate me for this. And I can't say that I blame you.

PAUL. What?

MANDY. Just let it settle before you say anything.

PAUL. What is it?

MANDY. I'm still taking the pill.

PAUL. *(Destroyed.)* What?

(Focus to BARBARA and MICHAEL.)

BARBARA. You missed the damned Christening. Of your own sister's baby. Your niece.

MICHAEL. I had a problem.

BARBARA. Do you have any idea how embarrassed I was to be there alone?

MICHAEL. I can't apologize enough for that.

BARBARA. That was the last straw.

MICHAEL. It was for me too. If you can believe it, I absolutely thought I was right at the time. I was angry at you, and I was angry at my sister for scheduling a baptism during the fifth game of the semi-finals.

BARBARA. And you think *I* was mad, your mother was ready to divorce you before I was.

MICHAEL. I've been seeing a shrink.

BARBARA. Come again.

MICHAEL. Yeah. Hard to believe, right? Mr. Macho sprawled on the sofa spewing his problems to a total stranger and a box of Kleenex.

BARBARA. What on earth –

MICHAEL. I missed you. I couldn't stop crying. Actually, the first month was kind of nice. I could do whatever I wanted without consulting a committee.

BARBARA. I was actually touched there for a nanosecond.

MICHAEL. Before I knew it, though, I would go to bed at night at start crying. Sobbing. The kind of cries you hear from teething infants.

BARBARA. Really?

MICHAEL. It was getting so bad I couldn't go to work. So I finally made the phone call.

BARBARA. How often do you see him?

MICHAEL. It's a her, actually.

BARBARA. My macho husband is seeing a female therapist?

MICHAEL. I'd requested a man, but there were no appointments available for weeks and I was getting tired of changing the pillow case every day – the salt in the tears wreaks havoc with the dyes.

BARBARA. You need to get a high thread count –

MICHAEL. And wash them separately in cold water. I know. Anyway, I went with what was available. Nice woman. I thought she'd just tear into me, but she was very understanding.

BARBARA. You know how to do laundry?

MICHAEL. Learned how to cook a few meals too. And get this –

BARBARA. What?

MICHAEL. *(He covertly scans the restaurant to be sure nobody's listening.)* I went clothes shopping on my own.

BARBARA. Michael. I'm so proud.

MICHAEL. Part of a twelve step program. Hello, my name is Michael and I'm afraid of Macy's. By the end of the week I'd bought two shirts and a pair of pants.

BARBARA. What kind of pants?

MICHAEL. ... Brown?

(Focus to TODD and DORIS.)

TODD. To tell the truth, I give any couple who enters into marriage a great deal of credit these days. There aren't a lot of positive role models out there.

DORIS. My parents stayed together, but they probably shouldn't have.

TODD. Mine divorced when divorce was still taboo.

(Focus on MANDY and PAUL.)

PAUL. I'm not sure I ever want to see you again.

MANDY. I understand if that's the case.

PAUL. I mean, this was an issue of trust. You told me you went off the pill and I believed you. If I can't trust you anymore, how can we have a relationship?

MANDY. Now you understand.

(Focus on BARBARA and MICHAEL.)

MICHAEL. — stemming back to my relationship with my mother.

BARBARA. Didn't I always tell you that?

MICHAEL. I told you so. Is that what you're saying? I told you so?

BARBARA. No, I said, "Didn't I always tell you that." Whole different accusation.

MICHAEL. You should try therapy yourself. It's good. Might help you to overcome that insatiable need to succeed.

BARBARA. Do you think? Is it helping you to overcome your insatiable need to fail?

MICHAEL. Very good. And the answer is yes.

BARBARA. Oh, really. How so?

MICHAEL. I don't want to sign those papers.

(Focus on TODD and DORIS.)

DORIS. No, I like that we see things differently. How boring would it be if we agreed on every subject?

TODD. Sure, it's endearing to differ on a first date, but see how endearing it is ten years from now.

DORIS. It depends on the disagreement. I really don't want to be married to someone who agrees with everything I say. That's a "yes man." I don't want a "yes man."

TODD. Yeah, you're right.

(Silent focus on MANDY and PAUL. MANDY removes her necklace and gently returns it to her husband, then exits the restaurant leaving PAUL alone at the table, dumbfounded. Focus returns to TODD and DORIS.)

DORIS. Uh, oh.

TODD. What?

DORIS. She left.

TODD. Who left?

DORIS. The couple. The one you said was having an anniversary. She left the restaurant. I think they had a fight.

TODD. Probably over something they found endearing on their first date.

DORIS. *(Distressed.)* Why even get involved in a relationship if there's a fifty/fifty chance it won't work out?

TODD. Because there's a fifty/fifty chance that it will?

DORIS. Great odds.

TODD. I think as the generations progress we're becoming more intelligent about whom we choose as a mate. We're becoming more selective, marrying later in life, and learning from the mistakes of others.

DORIS. You think?

(After sitting alone in quiet contemplation, PAUL drops some bills on the table and exits slowly as the DORIS and TODD conversation continues uninterrupted.)

TODD. As the culture changes, so too will the statistics. I wouldn't be surprised if some day in the near future the ratio of successful, long-term relationships is closer to two-thirds.

DORIS. I hope you're right.

(Two of the three tables are still occupied. BARBARA, who has been dialing a cell phone, brings it to her ear.)

BARBARA. Hello, Edgar —

(Blackout.)

END OF THE PLAY

SEATING ARRANGEMENT

Michael   Barbara

Paul   Mandy

Todd   Doris

PROPERTY LIST

The following props were used in the original production and may vary. The use of actual foodstuffs is left to the discretion of the director; eating may be pantomimed.

3 tablecloths
6 place settings
6 cloth napkins
5 wine glasses
1 rocks glass
2 water glasses
2 bottles of wine
3 bread baskets
2 menus

1 credit card
1 pen
1 checkbook with bill
1 necklace
4 plates of food
1 large Caesar salad
1 briefcase
1 set of divorce papers

COSTUMES

WAITER
    Black pants and white shirt, black bowtie, white apron

PAUL
    Dress pants and shirt, wedding ring

MANDY
    Skirt and blouse, wedding and engagement ring

MICHAEL
    Dress pants and shirt, jacket, tie, wedding ring

BARBARA
    Business suit

TODD
    Dress pants and shirt

DORIS
    Flower print dress

Lightning Source UK Ltd.
Milton Keynes UK
UKOW01f2019111017
310829UK00005B/279/P